Challenging Saber:
The Alliance Book 4

By S.E. Smith

Acknowledgments

I would like to thank my husband Steve for believing in me and being proud enough of me to give me the courage to follow my dream. I would also like to give a special thank you to my sister and best friend, Linda, who not only encouraged me to write, but who also read the manuscript. Also to my other friends who believe in me: Julie, Jackie, Lisa, Sally, Elizabeth (Beth) and Narelle. The girls that keep me going!

—S.E. Smith

Montana Publishing
Science Fiction Romance
Challenging Saber: The Alliance Book 4

First E-Book Published December 2015
Cover Design by Melody Simmons

Summary: A damaged alien warrior to fights to save the human woman he loves when she is caught behind enemy lines during a civil war.

ISBN: 978-1-942562-70-2 (Paperback)
ISBN: 978-1-942562-69-6 (eBook)

Published in the United States by Montana Publishing.

{1. Science Fiction Romance. – Fiction. 2. Science Fiction – Fiction. 3. Paranormal – Fiction. 4. Romance – Fiction.}

www.montanapublishinghouse.com

Synopsis

Sometimes it takes losing the one thing closest to a warrior's heart to wake the beast that lives inside him…

Saber, a wounded Trivator, believes he is no longer a fit warrior, much less strong enough to claim a mate. Scarred, he does everything in his power to push away the delicate human female he has fallen in love with. He knows that she deserves a warrior who can protect her, not one that will need her constant help.

Taylor Sampson may be human, but that doesn't make her weak. She and her two older sisters survived four years on their own after the Alliance made first contact with Earth. She is all grown up now and has her eye on the one stubborn Trivator that captured her heart seven years before.

Taylor has one last assignment on another planet in order to complete her schooling. Once she finishes, she plans to show Saber that he is the man she wants, but when civil war erupts she is trapped behind enemy lines. When Saber discovers that Taylor has been left behind, the warrior inside him refuses to think of her as collateral damage in a savage battle for power.

Journey to a lawless, alien world and discover what happens when the beast awakens inside a damaged Trivator warrior when the woman he loves is threatened.

Table of Contents

Chapter 1

Seven Years Before – Earth:
The Collapsed Parking Garage:

"This way," Hunter said in a quiet voice.

Saber nodded, staring at the dark crevice between the huge slabs of concrete. A curse echoed through his mind when he saw Hunter disappear into the opening. Sometimes he wondered about his friend's sanity. If it had been him, he'd have left the human woman to her fate.

A grimace crossed his face as he slipped through the hole and slid down the incline created by the collapse of the building. With a shake of his head, he knew deep down he would have done the same thing as Hunter did if a human female had risked her life to save him. It was bred into their species to protect those that were weaker, that included all females.

Over the last four years of his mission, he had met a few human women. Most of them had been pleasant, but overall, he found them to be either too demanding or too delicate for his tastes. That had led to many frustrated nights since his arrival on the planet.

He paused when Hunter glanced at him and held up two fingers, then a third. Stepping to the side, he and Dagger spread out while Hunter took the center. This was Hunter's mission; they were the support. His vision quickly adjusted to the darkness. His gaze narrowed on the dim light and the soft voices in the far corner. Hunter slowly moved off to search for the female that had helped him, leaving him and Dagger to deal with the other two. He watched as Hunter disappeared into the darkness before returning his attention to the two figures by the fire.

His eyes were immediately drawn to the figure of the youngest human. She wasn't quite a woman, but she wasn't a child either. What he did know was that she was in a very dangerous situation, and that ignited a flame of anger inside him that he had never felt before.

His eyes scanned the shadows of the parking garage for signs of any males. It was hard to tell from the scents in the air. He could smell fresh blood and the acidic smoke from the fire. The blood was the same as from the warehouse where they had tracked the female earlier. He knew that the female Hunter was seeking had to be here, it was just a matter of where.

He turned his gaze to search for Hunter. He caught a glimpse of his friend's shadow and knew that Hunter was in the mode that made his name famous. It wouldn't take long for Hunter to find his prey.

He glanced at Dagger. Surprise and amusement swept through him when he saw Dagger's intense gaze on the two females. Dagger had always been the most forceful and deadly out of the three of them. It wasn't like he or Hunter couldn't be put in that same category, it was just they didn't play with those that pissed them off before killing them. Dagger was known to draw out the deaths of those stupid enough to get under his skin.

Turning his gaze back to the two females, Saber felt a strange twist in his chest as he listened to them quietly talk. The little one was trying to take care of the other. His eyes swept over her tousled blonde hair and slender, almost fragile form.

Anger burned in him as he wondered why the females did not have a male or males to protect them. As a Trivator warrior, protection of a female within a family unit was top priority. If a warrior proved himself worthy, he would be gifted with a family of his own. All warriors hoped to one day prove they were strong enough to have an *Amate,* a mate, to carry on their bloodline and fill the empty space inside them.

Saber looked critically at the young girl's face. There was something about her in particular that pulled at those protective instincts, that made him want to shield her from the horrors outside. She was too young and delicate to be living this way.

He wasn't sure what Hunter's plans were for the other female, but he had a feeling that it would involve offering his protection. If Hunter did, then these two would also receive the same shelter and care. That meant that he and Dagger would protect them as well, since they considered Hunter more of a brother than a friend.

Satisfied with his reasoning, he decided that Hunter could protect the one he was seeking, Dagger obviously was focused on the welfare of the injured female, and that left him to care for the little one. A grin curved his lips. Since she was obviously the youngest and smallest, that meant his job would be the easiest. He could handle that.

He snapped back to the present when he saw Dagger motion for him to move forward. He nodded and stepped out of the shadows into the dim light of the fire.

A moment later, he realized that he might just have made the biggest error of judgment in his life. His mistake was thinking the littlest one would be the easiest to control.

He drew in a hissing gulp of frigid air as he bent forward. He was trying to keep his footing after the little hellcat with blonde hair nailed him in the stomach with an anything-but-fragile piece of broken concrete that lined the fire pit. She had thrown it underhand with enough force to leave him gasping for air.

He rocked for a moment, trying to push away the pain. He thanked the Goddess that she hadn't hit him a few inches lower. If she had, any hope of ever having a family would have been over. Straightening, he glared back at her defiant eyes.

Something tells me this isn't going to be as easy as I thought, he reflected, warily watching as she bent and picked up another fragment of concrete.

Chapter 2

"I swear, Hunter, if that she-creature bites, hits, or tries to escape one more time, I'm going to put her in a cage!" Saber growled, staring at the petite female standing behind his friend several hours later. "Why you little…!"

"Saber," Hunter grimaced, looking at his friend's murderous face. "She is a defenseless female."

Saber could see what Hunter couldn't. His hands curled into tight fists when she stuck her tongue out at him before giving him a self-satisfied smirk. He didn't care that she was under Hunter's protection. Saber was about to throw her over his shoulder and scare a little respect into her.

He rubbed his wrist. He was sure she had drawn blood this time. He wondered if he should have insisted that the healer examine her for any diseases instead of believing the medic on board the transport when he said that, except for being malnourished, the youngest one appeared to be healthy.

"I swear, Hunter," Saber started to say again before clamping his lips shut. "Go, check on the other females, I will watch over her," he finally said with a weary sigh.

"Are you sure? I could see if another warrior…," Hunter offered before giving Saber a strange look when a growl escaped his friend.

"Did he just growl?" The young female asked in awe. "What are you guys? That sounded just like a tiger. I heard one do something similar at the zoo. Does he need to be caged or something? He isn't going feral, is he? Ugh! I bit him. You don't think he has rabies, do you? Maybe he should be quarantined. My neighbor did that to a feral cat that she found in the woods near our house. Do you guys have those big pet containers?"

"Taylor," Hunter warned, glancing at Saber's red face. "Saber is fine. He is under control. Isn't that right, Saber?"

"Oh, I am under complete control," Saber said with a tight, sharp-tooth smile. "Just leave the little human to me."

"Thank you," Hunter said with a relieved smile. "I won't be long. I hope that the healer will allow me to bring both of her siblings back to my rooms."

"Take your time, we will be fine, won't we, Taylor?" Saber promised.

He stared over Hunter's shoulder. His intense eyes locked with Taylor's wary ones that gazed back at him with growing alarm. He rolled his shoulders and bent his neck from side to side, enjoying the feel of the crack that released the tension building inside him.

"Keep her safe, Saber," Hunter finally said, breaking the growing silence. "Her sister is my *Amate*. That means that Taylor and Jordan are now under my protection."

"I know what it means, Hunter," Saber growled, not taking his eyes off of Taylor. "I promise there won't be a single bruise on her."

Hunter nodded, glancing once more at Taylor before reluctantly stepping around the table in the nearly deserted cafeteria. Saber had to give Taylor credit, she didn't scream until Hunter walked out of the room. Still, he should have known it wouldn't be easy to catch her.

..*

Shewta, she's fast, and slippery, and..., he thought as he wiped the white gooey food matter from his face, *creative when it comes to escaping.*

"I am so looking forward to wrapping my hands around her little neck," he muttered under his breath as several warriors chuckled from where they were sitting and watching from the safety of a corner table. "Taylor, get down from there right now!" He ordered, looking at the top of the cabinets attached to the far wall.

"Why don't you try to make me, you... you moron!" She snapped. "I've got a bowl of...," she glanced at the orange mixture with a frown. "Orange goop and I'm not afraid to use it."

Saber flicked a piece of green food particle off his left shoulder as he stomped toward the metal cabinets. Right now, he was wearing just about every other color of food matter the cafeteria served. Why not add the last? He was going to need to visit a cleaning unit as it was.

"I won't hurt you," Saber promised, watching warily as the cabinet under her shook. "Taylor, that cabinet is not secured to the wall properly. Be careful."

"You're just...," Taylor started to say when the cabinet shifted under her. Her eyes widened in alarm when it began to tilt. "Catch me!" She cried out before slinging the bowl in her hand to the side and jumping.

The sound of the warriors shouting a warning was drowned by the loud crash of the cabinet as it fell. Saber ignored everything but the small figure flying through the air. His arms opened and he caught Taylor.

The force of the impact sent him backwards. On the second step, his left foot hit one of the items that Taylor had thrown at him. The combination caused him to lose his balance and he fell.

His arms instinctively wrapped around Taylor to protect her as his back hit the hard, tiled surface. He was surprised when he felt her hands wrap protectively around his head to cushion the back of it. It took a moment for him to draw in a deep enough breath to speak. He opened his mouth to give Taylor a piece of his mind, but he snapped it shut when he locked gazes with the bright eyes staring down at him in worry.

"Are you okay? I didn't mean for that to happen," she said in a breathless voice. "I... Thank you for catching me."

Saber's expression softened. The feel of her in his arms reminded him of just how small and fragile she was. He glanced over her shoulder and scowled at the grinning faces of the other warriors who had come to make sure that Taylor was unharmed.

"Is she alright, Saber?" Arrow asked with a grin.

"Yes," Saber grunted with a wince when Taylor pushed up on his chest and accidentally kneed him in the groin. "Careful, little one. I'd like to keep those intact."

"Oh, sorry," Taylor muttered, turning a little red as she climbed to her feet and stared down at him with a wiggle of her nose. "Boy, I didn't miss you much, did I?"

Saber grimaced when the other warriors chuckled. "No, you didn't."

"I was a kick-ass softball player before…." Her voice died and she looked around at the group of warriors towering over her before she turned her head to look back down at Saber. "I want to see my sisters," she said, wrapping her arms protectively around her waist.

The other warriors registered the change in Taylor from bubbly pain-in-the-ass to a somber young girl at the same time as he did. Saber rose to his feet, wiping a hand down over his side before he tentatively reached out and drew her into his arms. With a fierce glance at the other warriors, he jerked his head for them to leave them alone.

"It will be alright, Taylor," Saber murmured, holding her stiff body against his. "We will not harm you or your sisters."

Her arms slowly unfolded and she slid them around his waist, resting her cheek against his chest. That protective possessive feeling he felt the first time he saw Taylor swept through him.

"How can we be sure?" Her muffled voice asked. "Everyone else… I wish my dad were here."

Saber frowned at her fractured words. He wondered where the male was. Taylor and her two older sisters appeared to be alone, but what if they had protectors? He didn't know if Hunter or Dagger knew the answer to that question.

"Where is he? If you tell me, I will do everything I can to reunite you with your protector," he promised in a husky voice.

"You can't," she replied with a sniff. "He's… he's… dead. It's just Jesse, Jordan, and me now."

A shudder ran through Taylor, and Saber frowned when he felt her ribs through her threadbare shirt. She was too thin. The knowledge that his people and the Alliance were partially to blame for that fact did not sit well with him.

His species, the Trivators, had come to Earth four years ago. Their mission was to initiate first contact and prepare the Earth for inclusion into the Alliance, a vast coalition of planets that encompassed a large number of star systems.

They had encountered resistance before, but never like this. Mass chaos had reigned around the planet.

While the humans were all the same species, their beliefs and lifestyles went from one extreme to the other. Tribal groups, fanatics, those greedy for power and wealth, and those that refused to accept they were not the only ones in the universe fought against not only the Trivator forces, they fought each other too, until their civilizations crumbled.

Bending, he scooped her up in his arms. He glanced at where Sword, Edge, and Thunder were watching in silence. All three men had a tense look of regret on their faces. He bowed his head in acknowledgement. They couldn't change what had been done, but he could change what happened to Taylor. She would not only have Hunter to protect her, but Saber and Dagger, as well.

"You are not alone any longer, little one," Saber whispered as he carried her out of the cafeteria. "I will watch over you."

Neither one of them spoke as Saber turned left at the end of the hallway. They had been negligent about Taylor's welfare. He felt another shaft of guilt pierce him. Taylor's two sisters, Jesse and Jordan, had been critically ill while Taylor had been a fireball of rebellion. She had fought like a warrior trying to protect her sisters. Because of her resistance, it never dawned on Saber that Taylor might need medical attention as well. The medic had checked her over and said she needed food, but otherwise appeared healthy.

"Where are you taking me?" Taylor asked, not moving her head which was nestled just under his chin.

"To the medical unit," he replied in a gruff voice. "I should have insisted that the healer check you over."

"Is that where Jesse and Jordan are?" She asked, tilting her head back to look at him. "You have dried mashed potatoes in your hair."

A startled chuckle escaped Saber. "I think I have more than that. You hit me more than you missed. You have a very good aim for a female. You are also very…." He stopped as he tried to think of the right word to describe her quickness.

"I'm very what?" Taylor asked with a puzzled frown.

Saber glanced down at her as he paused outside of a dark green door. "Fast. You are very fast, but the way you could jump and flip… I'm not sure the correct human word to use," he said in frustration.

"I'm very limber," she replied with a small smile. "I was in gymnastics. I was really, really good at it. Dad…," her voice choked for a moment and her eyes glittered with tears. "Dad said I needed it because I was born with too much energy for anyone to keep up with."

"I'm sorry about your father, Taylor," Saber murmured, reaching down to open the door.

Taylor shook her head and snuggled up against him again. "It wasn't your fault," she whispered. "He was killed the first day by a human. We've been running ever since. I'm tired of running. So are Jesse and Jordan."

"You'll never have to run again if I have anything to do with it," Saber said grimly, glancing as one of the medics came forward. "I want a healer to check her."

The medic looked at the grim expression on Saber's face and gave him a sharp nod. "Follow me," he said.

..*

Taylor sat on the exam table and looked around the room. The medic had ushered Saber out of the room, telling him that he would have to wait outside in the front office. She glanced at the door, listening carefully. She could hear the quiet murmurs of the medic and another man.

She bit her lip in uncertainty. Jesse and Jordan had taught her the first year they were on the run to look for anything that they could use. Her eyes flickered to the medicine cabinet attached to the wall. They could always use the medicine once they escaped from here. Drugs were the second hardest thing to find out on the streets; the first was food.

She wiped her sweaty palms down her faded jeans. She would wait until after the doctor saw her, then find a way to hide a few things away. Her eyes jerked back to the door when it opened and a huge man walked into the room.

"Hello, human. My name is Carp. You were with the other two females that are resting?" He asked.

"Are they…," Taylor said, nodding her head at his question. "Are Jesse and Jordan going to be okay?"

Carp studied the tablet in his hand for a moment with a frown before he glanced up at her and nodded. "Yes, but it was a good thing the three of you were found when you were. Your sisters were very ill and one of them had several broken ribs," he said with a grim look. "How long have you been without protection?"

Taylor pursed her lips. "Jesse, Jordan, and I have been protecting each other. If you mean how long have we been on the run? It's been four years," she replied with a shrug, looking on curiously when he held up a small device. "What's that?"

"It allows me to scan your vitals," Carp replied with a slight smile.

"How does it work?" Taylor asked, glancing at it with a frown.

"It picks up your temperature, heart rate, and blood pressure," he explained, pocketing the device in his jacket before reaching for another strange piece of equipment. "Please place your hands on the surface."

Taylor cautiously lifted her hands and laid them on the dark glass. "What does this do?" She asked as a red light ran back and forth several times, causing her hands to tingle.

"It is taking blood samples and running tests on them. The results will tell me if you have the same virus that your sisters are suffering from, if you are anemic, as well as other tests," he said, pulling the flat glass toward him and studying it. "When is the last time you ate?"

"About half an hour or so ago," Taylor admitted. "It was the first time I've had that much in years."

Shaking his head, Carp set the scanner down and walked over to the medicine cabinet. Pulling out a key, he unlocked it before dropping the key back into the pocket of his jacket. He scanned the contents. He started when he realized that Taylor had quietly stepped up behind him.

"What's that?" She asked, pointing to a purple bottle.

"A vitamin supplement," Carp replied with a raised eyebrow. "Are you going to ask me what each vial contains now?"

Taylor glanced up at him with a mischievous grin. "Yep," she said. "I've always been fascinated with stuff."

"A few drops in water will give you strength as it replenishes the nutrients and vitamins you are missing. This one will kill any infections you might have. This one will seal a wound and enhance healing," Carp explained as he touched each vial.

"How do you guys know how to do all of this stuff?" Taylor asked in curiosity.

Carp picked up several vials and turned, motioning for Taylor to return to the examination table. He placed several drops from the purple vial into a glass of water before handing it to her. Taylor studied it suspiciously before sipping it. She was surprised when she felt a charge of energy sweep through her. Quickly drinking the rest of the water down, she handed the glass back to him.

"Can you tell me if you are feeling pain anywhere?" Carp asked, motioning for her to lie back.

"Not really," Taylor said with a shrug as she scooted back and lay down. "I've got some bruises from Saber, but that's all."

"Saber?" Carp said with a dark scowl. "He hurt you?"

Taylor snorted. "Only when I hit his hard hide," she growled. "The guy is built like a brick wall. You try hitting him and see if you don't end up with a bruise or two."

Carp's scowl dissolved and he chuckled as he shook his head. "No, thank you," he replied dryly. "I've participated in enough training sessions to know what Saber, Hunter, and Dagger are like. This will take care of your bruising. I suggest that you refrain from striking any more Trivator warriors in the future."

"Of course you'd say that, you're one of them!" Taylor retorted.

"I've requested clean clothing to replace your torn garments," Carp said, running the last of his scans and motioning for Taylor to sit up. "I'll inform Hunter that you and your sisters may return to his quarters with instructions to return in a few days for a check up to make sure all of you are well."

"Thanks," Taylor said, smiling as she sat up.

She watched as the healer walked to the door and opened it after a soft knock sounded. He turned with a stack of clothing in his hands. She slid off the exam table again and reached for them when he held them out.

"I'll inform Hunter you are here. Just come back out to the front room when you are ready," Carp instructed.

"I will. Thanks, doc," Taylor grinned brightly.

Carp gave her an uncertain look before he nodded and stepped out of the room. Taylor breathed a sigh of relief and quickly changed. She glanced at the door before walking back over to the bed where she pulled out the key and scanner she had slipped from his pocket and hidden under the pillow.

It didn't take her long to place all the vials into her old shirt that she had tied up to make a bag. Her fingers hovered over a gun-shaped item. It was the same thing the medic had used on Jordan and Jesse in the transport that had brought them here.

"It might come in handy," Taylor whispered under her breath as her fingers wrapped around it. "Always think ahead, like Jesse says."

Wrapping the items in her jeans, she straightened. Once she, Jesse, and Jordan were together, they could plan on how to escape. She paused by the door and pulled down the paper taped to the wall. It was a map of the compound. It would definitely come in handy.

Drawing in a deep breath, Taylor grinned. This was actually fun. They were healthy, had clean clothes, food, and medicine. Now, all they needed to do was escape. Taylor thought of everything she had seen as they were walking to the building. There had been a line of garbage trucks leaving. They were checked coming in, but not going out. It wasn't an ideal escape plan, but knowing how well these aliens could smell, it just might work.

Doing a little jig, Taylor opened the door and stepped out. She smiled at Carp when he walked by her. She took the opportunity to drop the key back into his pocket. He was just going to have to get a new scanner.

"Thanks again for everything, doc," she said.

Carp bowed his head in acknowledgement. "I have instructed Hunter to take better care of you and your sisters. Now that he has claimed one of them for his *Amate*, you are under his protection."

"Sure thing," Taylor agreed, not understanding what an *Amate* was and deciding it didn't matter, as they wouldn't be here long enough to find out. "Bye!"

She bit her lip when she heard Carp's muttered words as he turned. If he thought they were strange, he needed to spend a few weeks in the outside world. With a sigh, Taylor saw Saber rise as she entered the room. The adorable alien moron still had dried food in his hair.

Chapter 3

"Hunter, wake up," Saber growled, bending down over Hunter's inert body and shaking him early the next morning. He patted Hunter's face before glancing over his shoulder at Dagger. "Anything?" He asked.

"They went out the back window," Dagger replied, nodding to where Hunter was covered by a thin blanket. "How is he?"

"Out cold," Saber muttered, glancing at the discarded injector. "You'd better get Carp. Hunter is going to be furious enough as it is. I don't think waiting for him to wake up would be a good idea. It will just give those females more time to run."

Twenty minutes later, a very pissed off Hunter sat at the same table where he had been hours ago. Saber couldn't help the grin that curved his lips. It would appear his little human had struck once again. The smile quickly turned to a scowl when he realized where his thoughts had taken him.

She's not mine, he thought in aggravation. *Well, she is not mine yet, but she will be.*

"Saber!" Hunter growled again, pulling him back to the present.

"What?" Saber frowned as he glared across the table at Hunter.

"I asked how Taylor was able to get her hands on a sedative injector." Hunter asked with an accusing tone, glaring at him.

Saber shrugged and waved his hand at Carp. "How should I know? The medic and Carp would not allow me back into the examination room. Ask Carp, he is the healer, not me," he snapped defensively. "I told you she was a little hellion. I was covered in food by the time I left her with you."

Carp raised his hands in the air and shook his head. "I just checked her over like I was asked to do," he retorted when Hunter turned his irritated gaze on him. "Saber insisted that the young human be examined. It was just as well that he did. Her body was showing an increase in white blood cells, indicating that she was fighting an infection. I suspect she would have been as sick as her siblings within a matter of days. Her body was also depleted of essential nutrients due to her extended period of malnourishment."

Saber rose out of his chair and glared at Carp. "You didn't tell me any of that! You said she was fine," he growled.

"I said she would be fine," Carp corrected. "After you notified me of what had happened to Hunter, I checked the medicine cabinet in the room where I examined Taylor. She cleaned it out. I need to return to the medical unit. All I can say is good luck. I have a feeling all three of you are going to need it!" Carp bowed his head in farewell before he walked out of the door.

Saber winced when Hunter ignored Carp's departure and turned back to stare at him. He knew what Hunter was going to say. The problem was Saber didn't have an answer.

"Which leads me back to how the *shewta* did she get all of that past you?" Hunter asked bluntly.

Saber raised an eyebrow. "How did she knock you out?" He retorted, deciding being on the offensive was the better of the two options since he couldn't very well say he had been too busy trying not to make a bigger fool of himself in front of Taylor than he already had in the cafeteria.

"I don't think the how or why matters now," Dagger finally said, turning from where he was standing by the window looking out at the compound. "What matters is that we find them."

Saber watched as Hunter bowed his head and drew in a deep breath before he rose out of the chair. He returned Hunter's stare when he glanced back and forth between him and Dagger with a slightly confused expression on his face. Saber knew Hunter could hear the slightly possessive sound in his and Dagger's voices when they talked about the other females.

Saber was reminded of when they were boys. They often knew what the other was thinking or feeling without having to be told. When they were boys, they had taken a blood oath that they would always be there for each other. Finding the women wasn't just for Hunter, who had to find Jesse now that he had claimed her, it was for Dagger and Saber as well.

"Dagger's right," Saber agreed. "We need to find them. Hunter," he paused, glancing at Dagger before drawing in a deep breath and returning his steady gaze to Hunter. "I believe these females are different. I… As of today, I pledge my honor as a warrior to protect them as if they were my own. The little one, Taylor, she is far too spirited for her own good. I believe you will need all the help you can get in keeping her safe."

Dagger nodded his head. "I agree, though for a different reason," he admitted, looking at Hunter. "I stake my claim here and now, my friend. The one called Jordan will one day be my *Amate*. I swear on my life that I will protect her… as soon as I find her again," he added grimly.

"*Shewta*!" Hunter said, staring in shock at Dagger. "You are sure?"

Dagger flushed, but didn't look away. "Yes," he replied in a quiet voice.

Saber couldn't quite meet Hunter's gaze when Hunter turned back to stare at him. His eyes focused on the window where the girls had escaped. He moved from one foot to the other as the silence grew. Finally, in exasperation, he looked back at Hunter with a slightly tormented expression.

"She is young," Hunter replied in a soft voice.

Saber could feel his own face heat. "I know," he replied.

"It won't be easy. Something tells me that she will push you to your limits," Hunter continued.

"I said I know," Saber growled before turning his gaze to Dagger's amused face. "Her sister is young, too. You will have to wait as well," he pointed out.

"Yes, but not quite as young as the other, and she doesn't bite," Dagger chuckled before he sobered and a frown creased his brow. "At least, I don't think she does."

"I think it will take all three of us to keep them safe," Hunter replied with a grimace as he ran his hand over his neck, touching the spot where Taylor had injected him with the sedative.

"Then, I suggest we go find them," Saber said, rubbing his hands together. "I have a little demon to strangle."

..*

Two weeks later, Saber stood outside the transport Hunter had obtained for them to search for the females. They were near the former downtown area of Seattle. Abandoned buildings in various levels of destruction stood as a testament to the ravages done to the city since the Trivators' arrival four years before.

The destruction was not what Saber was currently thinking about though. No, at the moment he was thinking of all the ways he could throttle the three females. He released a tired sigh and stared down at the scanner in his hand.

Every time he closed his eyes, all he could see was Taylor's body lying somewhere out in the crumbled ruins. His eyes lit up with hope, then fear, before a dark, primitive rage swept through him when a new reading showed up on the scanner. Fifteen dots surrounded three.

"Hunter," Saber growled in fury. "Over here!"

Saber held the scanner out to Hunter before turning it to Dagger. Without another word, he attached it back to his belt and turned toward the alley leading in the direction where the figures were located. He broke into a run when he heard the sound of a scream. It was Taylor.

Saber, Hunter, and Dagger immediately assessed the situation when they reached the target area. Fifteen men circled the women. Rage unlike anything he had ever felt surged through him when he saw one of the human males strike Taylor across the face. As if in slow motion, he saw her collapse in the rubble-strewn street. The man bent over her and began ripping at her clothing.

"Kill them," he roared as he barreled through the men standing between him and Taylor.

Saber pulled his laser sword. He cut a path through three men before they were even aware that they weren't alone any longer. He sliced through a fourth man as he tried to scramble away, severing the main artery in the man's throat with a clean stroke.

The man kneeling over Taylor would not die so quickly. He sheathed his laser sword at his waist. Reaching out, he grabbed the man by the back of his shirt and lifted him away from Taylor's unconscious body.

"Hey, this one is mine…," the human started to protest before he saw who had grabbed him. "Oh, shit!" The male whispered, paling.

"Yes," Saber agreed, flashing his sharp teeth at the male. "*Soco ballast,* human! Now, you die… slowly."

Saber caught the man's hand in his when the human tried to strike him. He closed his fingers around the man's hand and squeezed. He could feel the bones breaking under his grip.

"No!" The man screamed, fighting to break free. "Help me, damn it!"

Saber shook his head. "There is no one left alive to help you this time, human," Saber snarled as he twisted the man's arm, breaking it with a sickening snap.

"Why?" The male blubbered. "Why? They're just a couple of bitches. Why do you care what we do with them?"

Saber grabbed the male's other arm when he tried to push him away. His fingers wrapped around the human's wrist and he quickly twisted it, breaking the human's other arm. Leaning in, he made sure the human could hear him before he died.

"A true warrior protects those weaker than he," Saber hissed out. "This female belongs to me, human. She is not a bitch. She is a fierce warrior who will one day be my *Amate*."

"I didn't know," the man cried. "Please, I didn't know."

Saber stared into the man's eyes. "What did you do when she asked for mercy?" Saber whispered as the sound of fighting faded behind him.

He watched dispassionately as the man's eyes widened when he realized there would be no reprieve. He released the human's broken arm and wrapped his hand around the man's neck. With a quick twist, he snapped the bastard's neck before tossing the male's body to the side.

Stepping closer to Taylor, he knelt down beside her and carefully drew her torn shirt closed. He could see the steady rise and fall of her chest as she breathed. His fingers trembled as he ran them over her temple and cheek where a fine line of blood stained her skin.

He tenderly ran his hands down over her body, checking to make sure that she didn't have any injuries that would prevent him from picking her up and carrying her back to the transport. Confident that it was safe to move her, he slid his arms under her and rose back to his feet.

He was shocked by how little she weighed. Turning, he glanced over towards Dagger who was holding Jordan. He watched in concern as Jesse turned on her heel and started to walk away. Gazing down at Taylor's pale face, he couldn't help but think she looked incredibly young and fragile. She also needed immediate medical attention. He strode over to Hunter and Dagger.

"Get them to the transport," Hunter ordered, glancing at Taylor's bloody and bruised face with regret. "I will meet you there."

Saber glanced at Jesse's stiff back as she walked toward an alley opposite to their entrance onto the scene. "She won't come willingly," he warned.

Hunter glanced at him before he turned away. "I would expect nothing less from her," he muttered as he walked away.

Saber glanced one last time at Jesse before he turned and strode back toward the transport. He would let Hunter and Dagger worry about the other two sisters. His main concern was for the one in his arms. She was his world, whether she realized it or not.

"Goddess, help me," Saber muttered as he carefully palmed the transport platform open. "Something tells me I am going to need it before she is old enough to claim."

***

Saber stood inside the medical unit once again, only this time it was on the warship heading toward Rathon. He refused to stay outside when Carp had asked him. Instead, he paced back and forth waiting for Carp to finish his examination of Taylor.

He stopped when Carp stepped back from Taylor's side. His gaze flashed to the tablet Carp was frowning at before returning to the healer's face. He scowled when Carp didn't immediately look up.

"Well?" Saber demanded, clenching his fists in an effort to not reach out and snatch the tablet out of Carp's hands. "Is she going to be alright?"

Carp looked up and nodded. "Yes," he replied with a deep sigh. "I don't think I will ever understand why the human males treat their females like this. I must admit, I am glad we have left their world."

"So am I," Saber admitted. "When will she wake up?"

"I'm awake," Taylor grumbled. "It's kind of hard to sleep with you pacing back and forth."

Saber immediately stepped around Carp and walked over to the bed. He stared down at Taylor.

Carp had healed most of the bruising, but there was still a small discoloring. He started to open his mouth, to ask her what she and her sisters had been thinking, before snapping it shut when her eyes filled with tears.

"Don't cry," he grunted out as a feeling of panic began to rise inside him. "Don't...." His voice died when the first tear escaped to course down her cheek. "*Shewta*! You are trying to rip my heart out, aren't you?"

He sat down on the side of the bed. In the background, he could hear Carp quietly leaving them alone. He opened his arms when Taylor sat up. A deep sigh escaped him when her shoulders began to shake with her silent sobs. He awkwardly patted her back before he lowered his head and tightened his arms around her and rubbed his chin against her hair.

"Jesse... Jordan," Taylor sobbed.

"They are safe," Saber murmured. "Why did you leave? You were safe at the compound."

Taylor pulled back to gaze up at him with watery eyes. He reached for a tissue on the tray next to the bed and held it out to her when she sniffed. He waited as she blew her nose and wiped her eyes.

"How were we supposed to know that?" Taylor asked stubbornly. "I heard Hunter say that Jesse was his *Amate*. I don't know what that is, but it doesn't sound good. We were going to try to head up to the cabin."

Saber gently raised Taylor's chin so she was forced to look at him. An amused smile curved the corner of his lips when she wiggled her nose at him and gave him a slightly suspicious glare. His thumb ran tenderly along her lower lip. He raised an eyebrow at her when she tried to bite it.

"Still trying to bite me, little one?" He asked with a soft chuckle.

Taylor's lips twitched. "You bet, old man," she retorted before falling back against the pillow. "I'm tired," she admitted with a huge yawn. "So, Jordan and Jesse are okay?"

Saber nodded, seeing the pleading look in Taylor's gaze. "I swear on my honor as a warrior," he promised. "Sleep, my little warrior. I will look after you and keep you safe."

Taylor rolled onto her side and gazed around the room with a frown. She rolled back over onto her back and gazed up at him. He could see the confusion in her eyes.

"Where are we?" She asked in a hesitant voice.

Saber reached over and tenderly brushed her hair back from her face. She relaxed back onto the pillow at his touch. Something told him that watching over her was going to be a challenge to not only his patience, but to his control as well.

"We are on the *Star Raider,*" he murmured. "We are returning to Rathon, where my home is."

"Oh," Taylor whispered before her eyes began to droop. "That's kind-of cool."

Saber watched as her eyelids slowly lowered until they created two crescent moons against her pale cheeks. Within minutes, her breathing had deepened and he knew she had slipped into a deeper sleep. He glanced toward the door when he heard Carp pause outside of it.

"Good luck, Saber," Carp replied with a slight grin. "I have a feeling you, Dagger, and Hunter are about to discover a battle that will take all your skills to win."

Saber glanced back at Taylor's relaxed face. Carp was probably right. One thing Saber knew, it was a battle he planned to win.

Chapter 4

Several months later, Saber stood in the shell of the home he was building. It had been a long and difficult journey back to Rathon. His lips twisted. If he thought that being around Taylor was difficult on board the warship, it was nothing compared to having her all to himself here in his home.

He walked over and stared out of the opening to the overgrown courtyard. His thoughts were on Taylor and the home he wanted to finish for her. She liked the garden at Hunter and Jesse's house. Once the house was finished, he would work on creating a similar garden for Taylor.

They had only been on his home planet of Rathon for a month and he could already feel the strain of being so close to Taylor, yet not being able to touch her. The fact that she was clueless of her effect on him only made the situation worse.

His eyes closed when he heard the familiar sound of the air bike she had talked Hunter's father, Scout, into giving her. Drawing in a deep breath, he turned just as the front door opened. For a second, Taylor's figure was silhouetted in the doorway. Saber swallowed when he felt his body's immediate reaction. Taylor was filling out in all the right places now that she was eating on a regular schedule.

She had recently celebrated her sixteenth year of birth and he swore her breasts had blossomed a full size as well. At least, it looked like it from the top she had on. His eyes narrowed dangerously.

"What the hell are you wearing?" He demanded.

Taylor paused at the entrance to the living room and grinned, turning in a circle before dipping into a deep curtsy. The mischievous grin that was permanently glued to her lips when she was around him lighted up her face. He couldn't help it. He really tried to keep his eyes on her face, but *shewta* if they would stay there. A silent groan escaped him when he realized that she was fully unaware of what was running through his mind.

"Do you like it? Hunter's mom, Shana, made it for me," she said in excitement. "It's been so hot lately and I was telling Shana about the halter tops that I used to wear and she had me draw out what one looked like. Yesterday, she took me shopping. She helped me pick out the material and she made it last night."

"That is nice… but, where is the rest of it?" He asked in a strained voice.

"You sound just like Hunter," she replied in disgust.

He studied her as she stepped into the room and dropped her backpack next to the unfinished wall. The groan that he had kept silent a moment ago escaped this time when he saw her long, tanned legs as she walked toward him. While her shorts weren't short, they were glued to her hips and thighs. If they were any tighter, he'd be able to… Another groan escaped him before he could smother it.

"Hey, it isn't that bad," she said with an easy grin.

His eyes flew to her face as she stepped up and wrapped her arm through his. She stared around the room before she focused on the overgrown garden. Saber began to recite the Trivator code of ethics when she curled her fingers around his hand and squeezed.

"What isn't so bad?" He asked in a hoarse voice.

"All this," she said with a wave of her hand. "Between the two of us, we can kick butt. What are we working on today?"

"The walls in the bedroom," he said.

Great! He snarled to himself. *It is obvious where my mind is at the moment. She's only sixteen. She's only sixteen. I promised Hunter I would give her until her twenty-first year. That's only another…*

"*Shewta*!" He muttered in defeat.

Five more years! I'll never survive, he thought to himself when she turned and bent to pick up the bucket of tools that he kept by the door for her.

"You're just being an old fuddy-duddy. Come on, I'll rub your muscles afterwards if it helps," she teased.

"I'm not an old fuddy-duddy," Saber muttered.

His eyes immediately went to her ass as she walked down the hallway. His body throbbed with need. It was going to be a long afternoon.

"How is your schooling going?" He asked in a gruff voice.

The smile on Taylor's face faded and she shrugged. "Okay, I guess," she mumbled. "At least I have Charma's grandkids going there, but they are in different classes," she told him, referring to Hunter and Jesse's housekeeper's grandchildren.

Saber watched in concern as she placed her bucket on the floor and pulled out a painting wand. Her cheerfulness had evaporated at his question. A scowl darkened his face and he reached over and took the wand from her hand before she could program it.

"Tell me," he ordered, staring down at her with a look that told her that he wasn't going to take 'nothing' as an answer.

Taylor pursed her lips into a pout that made him want to bend down and kiss that look right off her face. Of course, he didn't. He just really, really wanted to.

"It's just... I just don't fit in," she whispered as her bottom lip trembled and tears filled her eyes.

Panic hit Saber hard. The teasing Taylor, he could handle. The furious Taylor, he could relish. The crying Taylor? Now, that was enough to overwhelm even the strongest warrior's defenses. He started when she suddenly stepped close to him and wrapped her arms around his waist. He swallowed and wound his arms around her as she pressed her cheek against his chest.

"Why do you feel like you don't fit in?" Saber asked in a soft tone.

"The teacher is talking about all this technology that I don't know about. Heck, I'm still trying to learn the language," she sniffed. "He was asking questions about the different planets in the galaxy and specifics about the species. The only one I knew even a little bit about was the Trivators and he didn't ask about you guys. Then, the math class! Oh my God! I'm so stupid when it comes to math," she groaned. "I hate it, and the teacher there was talking about all these equations and theories and other crap. The only areas I'm any good at are the physical training and science classes."

"You are not stupid," Saber growled under his breath. He stepped back and slid his hands down her arms to hold her away from him when she tried to hide her face again. "Taylor, look at me," he ordered. He waited until she looked up at him before he spoke again. "You are one of the smartest females I have ever met."

She sniffed again. "I don't feel it," she mumbled in a grumpy tone. "The other girls…."

"What did the other girls do?" Saber demanded angrily.

Taylor looked away. "They make fun of the way I talk and how I dress and the way I look. One of them even called me ugly," she whispered, refusing to look at him. "I punched her in the nose."

"She called you… You did what?!" Saber exclaimed, placing his hand under her chin so she was forced to look up at him.

Taylor's lips twitched. "I said I punched her in the nose," she reluctantly admitted. "I was aiming for her mouth, but she turned at the last minute to say some other nasty comment to the group of girls she was with and I hit her nose instead."

A startled chuckle escaped Saber. "Did you make her bleed?" He asked in curiosity.

"Maybe a little," she said with a twinkle in her eye. "The teacher wanted to know what was going on. One of the guys in the class told him what she called me."

"Guys? Since when do they allow the males close to the females in the schools?" Saber demanded with a frown. "It was always forbidden for warriors in training and females to attend the same schools."

Taylor shrugged. "I don't know. Maybe it's because Buzz and the other guys aren't training to be warriors. Buzz said he wanted to go into medical training," she explained. "I was hoping I'd get suspended from school. Then, I could help you out more. Instead, the teacher complimented me on my defense and told the other girls that such behavior was unbecoming of a member of the Trivator species."

Saber shook his head. "You have the right to defend yourself," he argued.

"That's the same thing that Buzz said," Taylor replied with a sigh. "He's started helping me with some of my classes. That's why I was late today. We're meeting every afternoon after school for an hour and for two hours on the weekends."

"He… You are meeting another male after school?" Saber asked in shock, releasing her arms and stepping back so he could frown down at her. "Where? Is Hunter aware of this? Who is your chaperone?"

Taylor looked at him with a raised eyebrow. "You're kidding me, right? I mean, you aren't serious about needing a chaperone, are you? And, of course, Hunter is okay with it! Why shouldn't he be? Buzz is super nice and I think it is really sweet of him to not only stand up for me, but offer to help me with the classes I'm having trouble in."

"You are not allowed to be alone with another male, Taylor," Saber ordered in a firm voice. "It is not… proper."

Taylor rolled her eyes at him and shook her head. "That's what Hunter said until Jesse had a talk with him. He's cool with it now. It isn't like I'm interested in Buzz in, you know, *that* way," she added with a sigh. "Anyway, let's get started. Talking about school is depressing. I'd rather talk about other things."

"What do you mean by 'that' way? And what other things," Saber asked, frowning when she grabbed the painting wand out of his hand and danced away.

"I meant boys, of course," she said with a shrug. "Buzz is cute, but I'm not about to blow my relationship with him. I'd rather talk about what new ideas you have for the house. I thought about your idea of putting in a long pool in the central garden. Water features are always nice."

Saber's mind was still stuck on 'Buzz is cute'. He listened as Taylor talked about the different plants that Shana and Scout, Hunter's parents, had at their house, before she described the new ones that Bronze, Charma's *Amate,* was currently planting around Jesse and Hunter's garden.

..*

A week later, Saber stood in the same spot. He knew that Taylor was on her way. His gaze flickered to the tracking device he had placed on her air bike. After her comment about meeting with Buzz to study, he decided if Hunter wasn't going to monitor Taylor's whereabouts the way he should, then Saber would take over those duties.

The scanner showed that she was almost there. Turning, he patiently waited as the sound of her air bike resonated through the house. Time seemed to crawl to a stop as he waited for her to enter the house.

"Hey, Saber, I'm here," she hollered as she stepped into the house.

"I'm here," he replied in a quiet voice.

"Hey, what are we…," her voice faded when she saw what he was wearing. "You're leaving," she whispered, staring at him in shock.

"Yes, Dagger and I have been assigned a new mission," he said.

"When?" She asked, setting her backpack down on the floor and walking toward him.

Saber clenched his fists to keep from reaching out and grabbing her. Taylor had no idea that her every emotion showed what she was thinking and feeling. He didn't want her to know. He could see in her eyes what her heart already knew, but her mind had yet to register, that she belonged to him.

"In an hour," he responded in a rough voice when he saw the panic in her eyes.

"An hour! How long have you known?" She demanded.

"A week after our return," he admitted, wincing when a murderous expression crossed her face.

"Why didn't you tell me sooner?" She snapped, folding her arms across her chest and tapping her foot.

"I didn't want you to worry," he said, defensively. "Hunter… felt it best to tell you in person," he added.

"Oh, he did, did he? And, you thought waiting until an hour before you left was the best way to break the news to me? Where are you going? How long are you going to be gone? What am I supposed to do while you're gone? Argh! I can't believe you waited until an hour before you leave to tell me all this!" She angrily growled.

Saber turned and warily watched as she stepped around him and stomped out into the garden. Releasing a sigh, he followed her. He rubbed his chest when he saw her hand lift and brush impatiently at her cheek.

"I should have told you sooner," he admitted. "I just… I didn't want it to stop you from coming over."

Taylor sniffed and glared at him. "I'm going to paint your house pink while you're gone," she said.

A look of distaste washed across Saber's face. "Pink?" He repeated with a look of doubt on his face.

"Inside AND out," she replied with a mutinous nod.

"Ah, Taylor, I thought we agreed to use more natural colors," he reminded her.

"I'm also going to learn how to sew and put lace curtains up in the windows," she added, shooting him a piercing glare.

Saber swallowed. "The windows already darken automatically. Besides, I do not believe lace provides adequate coverage… though, if you think they are what you want, I guess they can be installed," he added hastily when her mouth tightened.

"I think gnomes in the garden would be good," she stated.

"Gnomes?" Saber replied in confusion.

"Nasty little beasts that throw mud at you and dig holes in your flowerbed, and steal your valuables," she replied with a nod and a wave of her hand at the tangled bushes.

"Gnomes," Saber repeated, looking at the garden with a grimace. "You are very upset."

Taylor turned and patted Saber's chest. "You haven't seen upset, yet," she promised, walking back into the house. "You'd better come back, old man. If you don't, not only will I come after you, I'll have carte blanche with your house until you do! Oh, one more thing," Taylor said, turning to stare at Saber.

"Only one?" Saber asked skeptically with a raised eyebrow.

His arms automatically opened when Taylor suddenly ran and threw her arms around his neck, hugging him like she would never let him go. He closed his eyes, holding her tightly against him. His hands moved down to her ass so he could pick her up. An intense craving flashed through him when she wrapped her legs around his waist and buried her face against his neck. He could feel her lips moving against his skin.

"I mean it, Saber," she whispered. "You'd better come back to me."

The powerful wave of longing struck him, and struck him hard. He knew without a doubt that he would come back. He had to; it was where he was leaving his heart. He was about to tell Taylor that when she bit his ear.

"Ouch! *Shewta*! What did you do that for?" He exclaimed, releasing her so he could grab his throbbing ear.

"For being such a turd about not telling me," she snapped, turning away from him. "If you ever do that again, I guarantee I'll come up with something a hell of a lot more painful," she warned as she bent and picked up her backpack. "You'd better come back, Saber!" She threatened before walking out the door.

Saber shook his head and massaged his stinging ear as a huge grin curved his lips. Taylor was staking her claim on him. He gently touched his ear, wondering if she had drawn blood again. Given how tender it was, she had definitely left her mark.

Chapter 5

"Hey, old man," Taylor said with a grin, two and a half months later.

Saber gave her that wary look that he seemed to always have on his face when she spoke to him lately. She knew why, too! It was probably all the pictures she was sending him of his house.

"I'm not that old. What have you done to the house now?" He asked, ignoring the chuckles of the men behind him. "Hold on a moment."

Taylor watched as Saber stood up. She caught a flash of what looked like the galley of the warship. In the background, she could hear the other warriors complaining to Saber.

"Hey, guys!" She called out and waved.

"Hello, Taylor!" The men yelled before they vanished and Saber's scowling face replaced the upside down hallway.

"You know they are enjoying this far too much, don't you?" Saber complained. "They are constantly teasing me now. It is very unwarrior-like."

Taylor rolled over onto her back and lifted the tablet in her hand. She laughed when Saber grinned back at her. Pulling the tablet closer, she pressed a kiss to the center of the screen.

"Does that make it better?" She teased.

Saber groaned and shook his head. She blinked when everything suddenly went dark. In the background, she could hear him curse before he muttered for the lights. It took a moment for her to recognize where he was sitting.

"Are you in a closet?" She asked, rolling again and looking down at the tablet.

"Are you rolling all over the bed again?" He retorted.

Taylor giggled. "Yes," she replied with a sigh. "I miss you."

Saber's gaze softened. "I miss you, as well, little warrior. How are your new classes going?" He asked.

"Better," she admitted. "I like this new school. The kids are nicer. Oh, did I tell you that Buzz transferred over this past week? He says their science curriculum is better than the old school."

"Buzz!" Saber snapped before he glared at the door when it opened. "I'm having a meeting!"

"My apologies, warrior," the man stuttered. "I just needed more cleaner."

Taylor watched as Saber reached behind him and grabbed a bottle off the shelf and handed it to the man. He ordered the man to shut the door before blowing a deep, frustrated breath. She shook her head at him.

"You know, you're in his closet. You might be a little nicer," she teased.

"There is very limited privacy on this warship," Saber complained. "Now, explain to me why this Buzz transferred to your school. I thought Hunter said you were doing better. Why do you still need Buzz around if you are doing better?"

"I am doing better, thanks to Buzz," Taylor retorted. "The school is nice, but it is really cool to have someone that I know there, too. I still get to see Charma and Bronze's grandkids, but it isn't the same. They have a busy life, and well, I'm still trying to figure out how to get back into the swing of things."

She knew that Saber understood what she was saying. They talked twice a week, the maximum amount allowed. She counted down the days until she could contact him.

"I'm proud of you, Taylor," Saber murmured with a sigh. "There have been a lot of changes in your life, yet you never give up."

Taylor propped her chin on her hand and gazed down at Saber. "Giving up meant dying back on Earth," she said in a soft voice. "Jesse, Jordan, and I swore we'd never do that, as long as we were together."

"So, what have you done to the house this week? Are the walls in my bedroom still that horrible neon pink?" He asked with a grimace of distaste.

"Nope, I changed it," she admitted. "How do you feel about purple? It's supposed to be the color of royalty, you know. Here's a picture of it."

She laughed when Saber groaned at the hideous, dark purple color. He was definitely going to hide the painting wand when he returned. She had no doubt about that. Ever since she discovered that all she had to do was point it at a wall, choose a color, and it would change, the inside of his house had been a virtual color wheel.

"I'm not sure I care for that color," he finally admitted. "I hate to say this, but the pink was slightly better."

Taylor released a sigh. "I thought so, too," she said.

"I see that you still have the curtains up," he commented. "They are very… womanly."

"You should see the garden! The Gnomes are multiplying like rabbits and have taken over the patio area," she warned, sending him another picture.

"You are right," Saber reflected. "They are nasty looking little creatures. I'll make sure I return home with all my weapons fully loaded."

"When are you coming home?" Taylor asked in a voice filled with longing. "I'm only working on the stuff I know how to do. Scout and Bronze have been helping some as well. I've got most of the garden cleared out."

Saber leaned back against the shelves. "Hunter, Dagger, Edge, and I are leaving for the planet tomorrow. If all goes well, I should return by the end of next month," he explained before he pursed his lips together. "Our time is up."

"I know," Taylor whispered, looking at the timer. "Be careful."

"I will," he promised.

"Oh, and Saber, I want you to know…," her voice faded and she bit her lip.

"What is it, Taylor?" Saber asked, a frown creasing his brow.

"I just want you to know that I love you," she whispered just as the signal cut off. "I love you, old man."

Rolling on the bed again, she held the tablet to her chest. She wasn't sure if he heard her confession of love. She hoped so. If he hadn't, well, she'd tell him again the next time she talked to him.

"Yep," she whispered, staring up at the ceiling. "You're mine, big guy."

..*

The next day, Taylor stood in the shadows of the kitchen, listening to the man who had come to the house. She could hear Jesse's soft denial and Shana's voice trying to soothe her. She couldn't hide any longer when she heard Shana mention Saber's name. Stepping around the bar in the kitchen, she walked over to stand next to Jesse and Jordan.

"If you would all have a seat, I will update you on the information I received on the way over," the man said.

Taylor reached down and gripped Jesse's left hand. She didn't want to sit down. She wanted to yell and scream. They had lost so much in their lives already. There was no way that life could be so cruel as to take the men that they loved away from them. Hadn't losing their mom and dad been bad enough? Hell, they had lost their whole world!

But, we found a new one, Taylor thought as she gazed around the table. *And a new family. Please… Please, don't take it away from us.*

"Unexpected fighting broke out in an area previously thought to be secure," the man said.

Taylor listened as he explained what happened. Deep down, she refused to believe any of them were dead. They couldn't be, especially Saber. She had just talked to him the night before. She had told him that she loved him. He couldn't be dead. He just couldn't. She glanced at Jordan before looking down at Jesse's pale face.

"What of Dagger?" Jordan asked in a barely audible voice.

Taylor glanced at Jordan again when the man answered. A searing numbness swept through her. She was wrong. Once again, Death had come to visit her family.

..*

Taylor sat on the swing outside. Her foot barely touched the ground, but it was enough to give her a small push as she stared up at the sky. She swore she'd stay there all night if that was what it took.

"What are you searching for, Taylor?" Scout asked, coming to sit on the bench that wrapped around the tree.

"A falling star," she replied, not looking at him for fear of missing it.

Scout turned on the seat so that he could see the stars. Taylor could hear the confusion in his voice. A sad smile curved her lips when he finally looked back at her.

"I'm afraid I do not understand how a star can fall," he finally admitted.

"They don't really," Taylor replied in a soft voice. "We call meteors falling stars back home. If you see one, you are supposed to wish upon them and if you are lucky, your wish will come true."

"Ah, yes, I am familiar with meteors," Scout said with a nod, turning to stare back up at the stars again. "And what would you wish for?"

"I can't tell you," she whispered, tears burning her eyes. "If I tell you, it won't come true."

She blinked rapidly when she saw Scout rise from his seat and walk over to her. She nodded and scooted to the side so he could sit down next to her on the swing. A trembling sigh escaped her when he wrapped his arm around her shoulders and began to slowly rock them.

"From the day I met you, you captured my heart," Scout admitted. "I love your sisters just as much, but you reminded me of all the things a warrior fights for."

"What do you mean?" She asked as she leaned her head against his chest.

"Jesse knows what it is to carry the weight of the world on her shoulders," Scout explained. "She is tough on the outside, but feels the pain for those that she believes she must protect alone. Jordan is different. In her eyes, I see the birth of the universe. She is an old soul. One who has lived over and over and over again, but who never quite forgot her previous life. She sees both the beauty and horrors in the world around her and fights to keep the balance."

Taylor swallowed. "What do you see when you look at me?" She asked in a soft, trembling voice.

"I see the birth of a star," Scout murmured. "I see beauty and passion and love. I see curiosity and innocence, but most of all I see a force that won't be denied what she wishes for the most. You are what a warrior fights for, Taylor. You are the hope for a better world."

"I love him," she whispered. "Oh, Scout, I love him so much that it hurts."

Scout hugged Taylor. "As he loves you, little star," he murmured. "Look! Make your wish, Taylor. Hold it close to your heart."

Taylor looked up in time to see a meteor streak across the sky. She held her breath and made a wish as it flashed across the heavens above. Biting her lip when it faded, she turned her head into Scout's chest and cried.

I wish that Saber would come home like he promised, she thought.

Chapter 6

A month later, Saber rose up, reaching for the light of consciousness, only to sink back down into the dark pit that refused to release him. The only rational thought that flashed through his mind was the knowledge that at least the unbearable pain was finally gone. Even that thought didn't last for very long.

It took him more than a dozen attempts to finally reach the surface. The first thing that came back was his hearing. He could hear the quiet voices. They sounded like they were far off at first, but each time, they came closer and closer. He was able to pick out a word or two that stuck in his brain, playing over and over like a broken vidcom.

"Shattered…"

"Should amputate…"

"Not worth saving…"

"No, you will…"

He heard Hunter's voice. His friend sounded angry. Another rumble of voices, but it was too difficult to piece them together.

"Live…"

"Maybe… Not sure yet…"

"I'm not leaving," a young voice said. "Get lost or I'll kick your balls to the next star system."

"I don't care! I know he can hear me," she argued. "I'll eat when I get hungry."

"No," he tried to argue, but his throat was dry.

He tried to lick his lips, but it took too much effort and he slipped down into the darkness again. It seemed like an eternity passed before he could find the strength to climb back up the slippery walls. He refused to give up this time. Someone was touching him. He could feel soft, smooth hands running up and down his leg. It took a moment for him to realize that he could actually feel the touch.

"My teacher showed me this technique," the voice was saying. "He said it helped with circulation and helped slow the deterioration of the muscles."

"Taylor, you've been here since early this morning," a soft voice chided. "You need to take care of yourself."

"I'm almost done," Taylor replied.

"Take...," Saber forced out.

The hands on him froze and were removed. A small moan escaped him when they disappeared. He moved his lips, trying to form the words.

"What?" A beautiful voice whispered next to his ear.

A sigh escaped him when he felt the warm hands touch his face. He instinctively moved his head. He wanted to feel them against his skin. He swallowed, trying to force some moisture into his throat.

"Take care... of... your... self," he finally forced out before the edges of darkness swirled around him again. He didn't want to sink back into the lonely pit. He wanted to break free and search for the face that belonged to the hands. "I don't..."

"You don't what?" The voice repeated.

"Leave me," he mumbled before falling backwards.

"I won't," she promised. "I won't ever leave you."

* * *

Eighteen months later:

"Boiling oil," Taylor muttered and held the pen to her lips and thought for a moment. "Naw, that would be a total waste of good oil."

Saber turned to glare at her. He gripped the arms of his airchair in an effort to keep from reaching out and wrapping them around Taylor's neck. She would probably continue to ignore him as he did it. She ignored everything else he did and said.

"You know, I can hear you thinking," he snapped.

Taylor looked up over her writing pad at him. "Spiders," she said, tilting her head. "How do you feel about spiders?"

"They are right up there with your gnomes," he retorted, waving his hand to the unfinished kitchen counter.

Taylor glanced over her shoulders at the dozens of strange little figurines that adorned the kitchen. She turned back and wrote something down. He snarled when she peered over her notepad at him.

"Goblins," she said with a grin, snapping her fingers. "I need goblins."

"How long are you going to continue to torture both of us with your insistence on coming over here every day?" Saber demanded, pressing the controls on his airchair until it stopped in front of her.

Taylor grinned at him. "Until you grow a pair of balls and admit that you like me coming over," she replied with a smile.

"You aren't going to go away, are you?" He finally muttered.

"Nope," she said with a shake of her head.

"Why?" Saber asked, staring at her in confusion. "Look at me, Taylor. I am half the warrior I was. I may never walk again."

"Wrong!" Taylor snapped. "Hunter might never have walked again. He was the one with the broken back. You! You had a busted leg. Even if you had both legs gone, you could still walk. So, why don't you get over your self-pity party, Saber? It's beginning to get a bit old. I'm ready for a new song."

Saber scowled at Taylor, but all she did was scowl back at him. He couldn't help it. His lip twitched. At first, he thought it was because he was mad, but the more they stared at each other, the more it twitched. He shook his head when the sound of a low snort escaped him. He meant it to come out as a growl, but it hadn't.

"You aren't going to make me laugh," he whispered with determination.

"I'll turn your bedroom pink again," she threatened, staring at him with a decided smirk on her face.

"I hate pink," he muttered, his lips twitching again. "And gnomes."

Taylor raised her eyebrow. "Wait until I add the goblins and spiders," she threatened.

"You are a cruel female," Saber hissed.

Taylor smiled and shook her head. "No, I'm not," she retorted in a quiet voice. "I'm a star who knows what she wants."

"And what is that?" Saber asked in a husky tone.

"I want my old Saber back," she whispered, staring into his eyes.

Saber's eyes shuttered and he pulled back on the controls. Turning around, he steered the airchair back in front of the windows. After several minutes of silence, he finally spoke.

"The old Saber is gone, Taylor," he murmured. "Go home. One day a warrior fit to protect you will come; accept him when he does."

He heard Taylor rise up off the lone piece of furniture in the house besides the bed in his bedroom. She walked over to him and pressed a kiss to his neck. He curled his fingers around the arms of the airchair to keep from pulling her into his lap.

"I'll see you tomorrow, Saber," Taylor whispered in his ear before she straightened and walked back to collect her belongings. "Oh, and for the record, I've already picked the warrior I want. He just needs to get his head out of his ass long enough to realize it. Bye!"

Saber didn't say anything. Releasing the breath he had drawn in, he reached up and touched the spot on his neck that he swore felt like it was burning. Dropping his hand back down, he turned the airchair toward the one room that Taylor hadn't been in. The door opened as he drew close.

Inside was a training room that he had installed while Taylor was in school. Pulling the chair up to the side of one of the benches, he slowly scooted forward and grabbed the bar along the side. He pulled himself up, forcing his shaking good leg to remain stiff until he could turn and sit down.

"Spiders," he whispered with a chuckle as he began his nightly workout. "I really hope she wasn't talking about real ones."

Chapter 7

Present day:

"I'm going over to Saber's house. I might be back later," Taylor hollered as she grabbed her jacket and slid it on before picking up her backpack.

"Taylor, are you sure you should?" Jesse asked with a worried smile. "I overheard him telling Hunter to keep you away from the house."

Taylor rolled her eyes and shrugged. "Okay, then I'm going down to the Quikie Mart for an iced coffee," she said.

"Where is this Quikie Mart? I have never heard of it," Hunter said, walking up to wrap one arm around Jesse and their five-year-old son, Lyon while holding one-year-old Leila in his other arm.

"Quikie Mart! Quikie Mart! I want to go to the Quikie Mart!" Lyon demanded.

Jesse snorted, drawing a giggle from Lyon who reached for her mouth. Taylor's expression softened at the lovable little boy who had the entire household wrapped around his small fingers. Pulling her hair out from her jacket, she leaned forward and pressed a quick kiss against Lyon's soft cheek.

"That's because those were only on Earth," Jesse responded in a dry tone. "She's going over to Saber's house."

Taylor could feel Hunter's eyes narrow on her stubborn expression. She didn't care what he said, she was going – period. She was an adult now. She didn't need to ask his permission to do anything.

"Taylor," Hunter started to say, but stopped when Taylor turned away.

"He needs me, Hunter," Taylor said in a quiet voice. "You know it and so do I."

Her shoulders relaxed when she heard his sigh of resignation. A smile tugged at her lips. That was what she loved about the Trivators, they were big bad teddy bears when it came to the women they loved. She knew deep down that Saber loved her. He just needed to understand that she loved him back to the very core of her soul and wasn't going to give up on him because of his own stupid misconceptions of 'not being a whole warrior'.

A wave of longing sent an avalanche of feminine power through her. She had felt his reaction to her. His mouth might be saying one thing, but his body was definitely saying something different.

"Good luck," Hunter finally said with a hint of amusement in his voice. "He can be very stubborn."

Taylor nodded. "So am I," she retorted with a grin. "Don't wait up."

"Taylor," Jesse said again in exasperation as her little sister walked out the door. "She's playing with fire," she said, turning to glare at Hunter with a pointed look.

Hunter gazed down at his *Amate* with a soft smile. "And she is very good at it. She is right. He does need her, whether he is ready to admit it or not."

..*

Taylor jogged down the front steps and over to the small transport that Hunter had given her for her twenty-first birthday. She threw her backpack into the passenger seat and slid into the driver's seat. Pulling the straps over her shoulders, she clipped the communications control onto her collar. With the expertise of hundreds of hours of flight time gained over the past two years, she pressed the power and rose into the air.

Glancing down at the house below, she couldn't help but feel a little sentimental. It had been her home for the past seven years. It was hard to believe that so much time had passed. Her life back on Earth seemed more like a dream than a reality.

Turning her focus back to where she was going, she had to admit she was happy that it had. The people on Earth were slowly rebuilding, according to the reports she was reading and conversations with Razor, Hunter's older brother, and Kali, his human wife…

Or Amate, Taylor thought as she flew over the thick forest below.

Still, Earth had a long way to go and a lot of rebuilding to do. A reluctant smile curved Taylor's lips as she flew a path that she did twice a day; once in the morning and once again every evening. Saber might be moody as hell most of the day, he might give her hell for coming every morning to bring him breakfast or give her the cold shoulder every evening, but he never told her to leave, not anymore. No, he could tell Hunter to tell her not to come, but he never told her because he knew she would just ignore him if he tried.

A part of her acknowledged that she had fallen for him the first time she saw him. They'd had their issues. He called her a kid, she called him an old man, but the constant banter back and forth had kept her going in the strange new world she'd found herself in.

Taylor sighed as she thought of everything that they had been through over the past five years. One of the most painful things was waiting for her to grow up. She would have accepted him at sixteen, but deep down, she reluctantly agreed that Hunter, Jesse… and even Saber, had been right. She needed time to grow up and learn more about her new life. Of course, she wouldn't have admitted it, at least not then.

Her life had changed and she'd found her focus almost five years ago. It had taken the near death of Saber and Hunter during a mission to give her life the inspiration and focus she needed. Hunter had received a severe spinal injury that almost paralyzed him while Saber had been critically injured to the point the healers were unsure whether he would live.

Saber required numerous operations, the last one just two months ago, to put him back together. The damage had been unbelievable. His right leg had suffered most of the damage. His upper thigh bone had been shattered; the muscles and nerves shredded as well as dozens of other hairline fractures. In addition, a deadly infection had set in by the time he and Hunter were rescued.

Five years later, he could now walk without his cane – most of the time, but he needed it when he was tired. He was still in a lot of pain which is what concerned Taylor. The constant nagging pain was evident by the permanent lines around his mouth and the shadows under his eyes.

Taylor knew the physical therapy was helping him. Every morning she would bring him breakfast and sit with him, chatting about her classes, what she was learning, and anything else she could think of until he finished. Then, she would start working on his leg.

He had balked at first, but she had persisted, refusing to leave until he did it. The first year afterward had been a trial. Saber had refused to do the physical therapy the healers had ordered. It took a while, but she discovered the reason was that the bone was not healing properly and it was excruciating.

She glanced down at the ground. She was almost there. Saber lived off the beaten path, almost thirty kilometers outside the town of Trivas. She was surprised the road leading to it hadn't been renamed Taylor Way. She had definitely made the journey enough times over the years to have it renamed after her.

She and Saber had worked on the place before his injuries. Of course, he hadn't been able to work on it the first year while he was in the hospital. She had spent most of her time with him there, until his release. After his discharge, it had taken almost six months before he would finally restart the work that needed to be done. He had withdrawn into the house and tried to become a hermit. Unfortunately for him, Taylor was just as determined that he rejoin the land of the living, even if it meant she had to pull him back into it kicking and screaming. Eventually, they began working on the construction of the house again.

She decided it had been good therapy for both of them. It had helped them work through the changes in their lives and given her the direction she needed to make her career choice of being a Physical Therapist with a focus in Developmental Research. She wanted to help those with extensive injuries like Hunter and Saber.

Now, after five years and her persistence, it was almost complete… with a few additions of garden trolls, gnomes, and other incentives whenever he was being a bonehead to her. It had become a running joke with them; he makes her mad, she creates something straight out of a Halloween movie to get back.

Or I change the color of the house on him when he isn't looking, she thought with a mischievous grin.

"Okay," Taylor breathed out the breath she was holding. "I hope tonight goes well. The big oaf better not start cheering when I tell him my news, otherwise he might need to be in traction again."

She guided the transport over the trees and gently touched down in the front courtyard. She shut down the engine and unclipped the straps. Opening the door, she grabbed her backpack before sliding out. She shut the door and walked around the transport just as the front door opened.

Her heart skipped and she felt the familiar warmth spread through her. The desire for him had grown hotter and stronger the older she got, and right about now, she was ready to rip Saber's clothes off and have her wicked way with him. She just needed to figure out a way to do it since he was a good head and a half taller than her.

"Hey," she said with an easy smile.

"It's late," Saber replied bluntly. "I thought you'd finally taken the hint and decided not to come."

Taylor walked up the steps to the house and patted Saber on the chest as she walked by him. "Ha-ha. You have the coolest sense of humor," she remarked with a mischievous grin. "Did I ever mention that I find that incredibly sexy?"

Saber's moody expression flashed to one of pure panic before he covered it with the mask he thought hid his true feelings. What he didn't realize was that Taylor could see the little nerve in his jaw pulsing. Once she had him under her, or over, whichever way he wanted to start, she might tell him about it.

"You know I don't like you returning to Hunter and Jesse's house after dark," he grumbled, following her into the house and shutting the door behind him.

Taylor nodded and flashed him another smile. She walked down the wide hallway into the living area. She loved this room now that it was finished. It was huge with curved walls that rose up to reveal a series of clear panels that on command would go from clear to shade to complete darkness. The back wall was actually a series of doors that opened all the way and disappeared into the walls on each side so the room became part of the outer garden. In some ways it was similar to Hunter and Jesse's house, but this one was brighter, more open and gave her a sense of peace.

"I really love this room," she said with a sigh, turning to face him.

"I know," Saber replied, moving to relieve the pressure on his bad leg.

Taylor's eyes immediately noticed the move. "Have you been doing your exercises?" She asked, dropping her backpack next to the couch and kicking off her shoes.

Saber scowled at her. "Yes," he bit out in a rough tone. "It's just a little stiff today."

"Let me take a look," she ordered, waving to the couch.

The scowl on Saber's face turned even darker. Taylor could tell he was going to argue, he always did. It had become a routine for them. What he didn't know was tonight was going to be different if she had any say in the matter – which she always did.

"I said I was alright," Saber growled even as he walked toward the couch.

"Lie down and let me take a look at it," she said, noticing that his short hair was still a little damp from his shower. "Did you take a hot shower or a cold one?"

"A cold one," Saber grumbled, sitting down on the edge of the couch and turning to lie down on it. "I knew you were coming."

Taylor chuckled and raised an eyebrow at him. "Is that because I make you all hot and bothered, old man?" She asked as she knelt on the floor next to him.

She carefully removed the thigh to calf brace he wore and set it on the floor next to her. She studied the long scars that zigzagged down his leg. Most wounds could be healed with minimum scarring; only the worst ones could not. Saber's leg reflected the devastation of damage done to the bone, muscle, and nerves. Two newly healed incisions caught her attention. They hadn't been there this morning.

"I'm not that old," Saber defended with a reluctant curve of his lips. "Yes, you make me hot. I want to wring your neck for not listening to me."

Taylor ran her hands tenderly over the scarred skin of his right leg. She could feel the knots in the muscles. Using a combination of her weight and pressure, she worked on each one. A low hiss escaped Saber when a particularly tight one released. Almost immediately, she could feel his body melt back into the couch. Her magic touch, as he liked to call it, was working.

"Leila has another tooth," Taylor said, knowing that talking often took Saber's mind off of what she was doing.

"She already had a mouthful," Saber said in a tight voice.

"Jesse said it is her two-year molars, I think," she said, rubbing his hot skin. "Lyon is learning to climb. Jesse and Hunter have to watch him like a hawk."

Saber frowned and glanced down at Taylor. "A hawk?" He asked in a husky voice.

"Yes," she murmured, getting lost in the feelings she got whenever she touched him. "It's a type of bird of prey back home. They have incredible eyesight."

Taylor glanced at Saber when she felt him stiffen. "You still think of Earth as your home?" He asked with a frown.

Taylor looked down at where her hands were working the muscle of his calf and shook her head. She would always think of Earth as her home, but it wasn't where she wanted to live any more. No, her place was here, in this house, beside Saber. That is where home was now.

"No. It will always be 'home' as in the place I came from, but it isn't my home anymore," she reflected, pausing to look up at him. "This is my home now."

Her eyes locked with his as she tried to convey that she wasn't talking about Hunter and Jesse's house or the planet in general, but this house. She knew he understood when he broke the contact between them and laid his head back and closed his eyes, shutting her out. She returned her attention to his leg, moving up to his upper thigh.

Her hands moved over the thick rope of muscles and smooth skin. He was wearing his shorts. Whatever he said, the evidence pointed to his hope that she would come because he normally wore a pair of low hanging jogging pants he had picked up on Earth when he was working on the house.

"How did the painting go after I left this morning?" She asked in a soothing voice, pausing and pressing her weight down on a hard knot. "Did you get it finished?"

"Yes," Saber replied in a clipped voice.

"What are you working on next?" She said, slipping her hands higher until they disappeared under the edge of his shorts before moving them back down along his thigh.

"The lighting," he muttered in a slightly hoarse voice. "I finished the wiring as well. I just need to install the rest of the fixtures."

Taylor rose to her feet. Not pausing, she quickly pulled her shirt off and tossed it to the floor. She had left her bra off after her shower.

She crawled between his parted legs with slightly trembling limbs. This was a routine he was familiar with from past sessions. In order for her to work on his upper thigh, she needed to use more of her weight. She leaned forward and began working on his thigh again before he could realize that this time it was going to be different.

A wicked sense of pleasure flooded her at the feel of the cool air on her breasts. She had purposely worn loose fitting pants and no panties. Her eyes moved to the evidence that he tried to hide, but couldn't. The material did little to cover his arousal.

"What will you do after that?" She asked in a husky voice.

"The gardens. I… I thought I would work in the gardens," he whispered. "I want to add some water features. I like what Hunter and Jesse did in their garden. I have some ideas that I'll show you later."

"I'd like that," Taylor whispered, leaning down and pushing her hands further up his leg and under his shorts all the way to his hip. "You can tell me about it – later."

A light groan escaped Saber before he could smother it. He just nodded his head once. Taylor knew he was highly aroused by the feel of her hands on the sensitive flesh of his hip. Pulling her left hand out, she ran it up his right leg. This time, she didn't stop.

A shudder ran through him when he felt her hands sliding up both of his thighs to his hips. She could feel the moment he was aware that this session was different. The fact that her lips were making a trail up the inside of his right thigh along the scar from his surgery might have been his first hint.

His breath hiccupped and his eyes flew open. He raised his head just far enough to lock eyes with her. She figured seeing that she wasn't wearing a shirt was his second clue that she was doing more than a therapy session.

"I love touching you," she whispered just before she wrapped her right hand around his swollen cock. "Damn, but you are one hell of a handful."

Chapter 8

Saber laid on the couch, soaking in every precious caress of Taylor's hands. Every time he closed his eyes, he would think of them as they worked his damaged muscles. The thing was, in his mind, he wasn't damaged anymore. He was whole, a fierce warrior that could take her, claim her, as his *Amate*.

For a few exquisite moments every morning and evening, he could pretend that he was worthy of loving someone as beautiful as Taylor Sampson. He could forget about the constant pain and stiffness that plagued him. Sometimes, by the end of the day, the simple task of cleaning up after a day's work became an almost overwhelming task. That was one reason that he refused to allow Taylor to stay late. He didn't want her to see that his leg often gave out, or his need for the cane that kept him from falling on his face.

His throat tightened when she ran her hands higher. He had to fight to keep the groan from escaping him. Her fingers were long and strong. He could just imagine them wrapped around him.

Sweat broke out on his brow when he felt her hands slide up under the edge of his shorts. It was taking every ounce of his self-control to focus on the questions she was asking him about the house.

"The garden," he muttered hoarsely, trying to keep his thoughts on what he was saying.

"You can tell me about it – later," Taylor whispered.

He heard her, but the words didn't register. Her hands had moved up his thighs to his hips and his brain was short-circuiting. He hoped to hell she didn't ask him anything else because he honestly didn't think he could answer her.

His eyes snapped open when her left hand moved up his good leg all the way to his hip once more. Only this time instead of moving down again, her left hand gripped his hip while her right hand… a choked gasp escaped him in surprise.

His head snapped up and his blazing yellow-gold eyes locked with Taylor's dark brown ones. She stared back at him with a combination of desire and defiance. His eyes widened when he saw her bare shoulders.

"Goddess, Taylor," he breathed.

The sexy smile on her lips sent his senses spiraling out of control. His eyes fastened on her lips as her tongue peeked out to run along her bottom lip. A choked moan escaped when she squeezed him before sliding her hand up to the tip of him and back down.

"Tonight, I'm not leaving," she informed him with eyes of melted chocolate.

"Taylor," he groaned, trying to shake his head in denial even as his arms reached for her.

A low snarl escaped him when she pulled back and slid off the couch. His eyes narrowed when she raised her arms to her hair. She pulled the clip holding it back free, and tossed it on the low table before running her hands down her side to the top of her dark blue pants.

"I want you, Saber," she said as she pushed her pants down and kicked them to the side. "I think I fell in love with you the first time I saw you."

"You hit me with a piece of concrete," he said, slowly sitting up. "You threw food all over me."

A mischievous smile curled her lips. "You caught me," she said, holding her hands out to him. "Catch me now, Saber. I need you."

Saber swallowed as he reached for her hands and stiffly rose to his feet. He blocked all the voices in his head that were demanding that he stop and think of the consequences. He pushed all the logical reasons he should resist to the darkest recess of his mind.

"Taylor, are you sure?" He demanded in a rough voice. "Once I touch you…." He shook his head and reached a slightly trembling hand to touch her cheek. "I don't think I'll be able to stop."

Taylor's laughter warmed the air, surrounding him. He closed his eyes when he felt her release his hand and step back. They popped open again in shock when her hand grazed the front of his shorts.

"I don't plan on letting you, big guy," she whispered huskily, turning and walking through the living room and down the hallway.

Saber's eyes darkened to a blazing gold as he watched the seductive sway of her hips as she walked toward his bedroom. Her long hair flowed around her shoulders, making him want to reach out and tangle his hands in it. A piercing shaft of hot need, so powerful he swore he felt like he would be lucky to pleasure her before he spilt his seed washed through him.

"*Goddess,* I love that female, but she drives me crazy," Saber muttered under his breath as he followed Taylor down the hall.

He would try one more time, while he still could, to convince her that this was a very bad idea. His hands curled into two tight fists as he tried to talk himself into remembering all the reasons that he had sworn he couldn't be with Taylor. In fact, he had decided earlier today that he would tell her tonight not to come back.

Drawing in a deep breath as he felt a small measure of reason return to his mind, he turned the corner into his bedroom. A low grumble of pleasure escaped him at the view of her kneeling on his bed, staring at him with a soft expression. He paused briefly, before taking a slow step forward. His hands reached for the bottom of his shirt. Ripping it over his head, he tossed it to the side. His hands went instinctively for his shorts. He pushed them down, pausing only long enough to step out of them before he walked slowly toward the bed.

He started to raise his bad leg, stopping with a grimace when he felt the muscles protest. Regret flashed through him. Even the joy of making love was dampened by his limitations.

"Don't," she whispered, leaning forward and cupping his face between her hands. "Touch me. Feel only me," she instructed, running her hands down over his shoulders.

Saber swallowed and nodded. He turned and sat sideways on the edge of the bed. His head turned toward her, seeking her lips. Taylor's warmth engulfed him as she slowly pressed him back against the pillows. She briefly moved down to gently help him raise his bad leg onto the bed before moving back next to him.

His body arched when he felt her slide one silky leg over his stomach. His hands instinctively rose to steady her as she straddled him. He could feel the heat of her womanhood pressed against him. Another curse escaped him when she slid lower and he felt his cock brush against her ass.

"Taylor!" He growled, gripping her arms tightly. "I've wanted you for too long to play… Goddess! Where did you learn that?!" He demanded hoarsely.

Taylor had pulled one hand free and was sliding it down between them. She wrapped her hand around his cock, holding it steady so she could brush the tip through her damp curls to show him he wasn't the only one who had been waiting.

"I've taken my fair share of medical classes," she reminded him. "It isn't all that complicated to figure out what feels good and what feels… great!"

Saber jerked when she slowly moved down his body. A loud groan escaped him at the feel of her lips against his skin. His hands fell to the bed and tangled in the covers to prevent him from wrapping them in Taylor's hair.

Another shudder shook his long frame. Her hair, it was brushing against his skin like a soft feather, making his skin so sensitive, he was afraid he was going to embarrass himself. His legs fell apart as she continued on her determined path to his…

"Holy Goddess above!" Saber choked out when he felt Taylor's warm lips lock around the head of his cock. "You'll be the death of me, Taylor!"

Taylor giggled and slid her mouth further down his length, causing his head to fall back as an explosive wave of pleasure crashed over him. His fingers twisted the fabric of the covers as a loud groan escaped him. This was something a Trivator female would never do. Their species was born with sharp teeth, making this something that most males would be very hesitant to even think of trying.

"Taylor," Saber hissed, trying not to move, but finding it impossible to keep his hips still. "I… This is too much."

A gasping shudder escaped him when she released him with a loud smacking sound. His eyes opened and he stared at her. In that moment, he knew he was forever lost to the power of his love for her. She was looking at him with liquid eyes filled with triumph and desire. Her hair fell over one bare shoulder and down to shield her beautiful breast.

"Come to me," he whispered, releasing his grip on the cover to hold his hands out to her.

A brilliant smile curved her swollen lips as she crawled back up his body. He slid his hands down along her side, enjoying the feel of her smooth skin against the roughness of his palms. The moment she straddled him again, he pulled her down to capture her lips with his.

Saber caught Taylor's soft moan when her lips parted. His tongue swept in, dueling with hers before running along the smooth edges of her teeth. His cock was straining, throbbing as he remembered her lips wrapped around him. Pulling back, he stared up at her flushed face.

"I need you," he admitted in a harsh voice. "I've never felt such a need before. You fire my blood, Taylor."

Taylor smiled down at him, pushing up onto her knees. He didn't resist when she pulled his hands to her small, but firm breasts. Her nipples were hard and swollen, begging for him to taste each sweet bud.

"I'll have to remember that whenever you become thick-headed," she said, throwing her head back when he pinched her sensitive nipples. "Oh!"

Saber's eyes darkened at her response. Her hips were moving back and forth in a restless ride. He could feel the heat and dampness against his flesh. She rose up and tilted her hips. He knew what she wanted and he couldn't have denied either one of them if his life depended on it.

He kept his eyes locked on her face as her head bowed. She stared back at him as she reached down to help guide his cock to her liquid core. Her face flushed when he pushed forward past her soaked curls. The bulbous head of his cock sank slowly into her as she relaxed against his hard length.

"Goddess, Taylor, you are so beautiful," Saber whispered, watching her face in awe.

It was true. Her face was flushed with passion and desire. He worried that he would hurt her. She felt so tight.

His eyes widened when she leaned toward him and gripped his shoulders. Her hair fell forward, creating a curtain around them. Her lips trembled as she drew in a deep breath, her body tense for a moment before she released the breath she had drawn in.

"I love you, Saber," she whispered, relaxing her thighs and sinking down on his cock as far as she could go.

Saber opened his mouth when he saw the flash of pain in her eyes and heard her smothered cry. Her hands curled against his skin, but she never looked away. He held his body still until he felt her begin to move. His hands slid around her waist, pulling her down onto his chest so he could roll with her.

A low whimper escaped her when he started to pull out, but he captured it. He wasn't going to leave her, not yet. His body trembled as he began moving in slow, measured thrusts. He wanted to give her enough time to adjust.

He released her lips when she raised her legs and locked them on his hips, her heels pressing into his buttocks. Rising up slightly onto his elbows so he didn't crush her, he pressed forward as an intense pleasure swept through him.

"I can feel you," he murmured, bending to rub his nose against her cheek. "I can feel every delicate, beautiful inch of you as you wrap around me."

Taylor's hands rose to cup his cheeks. She raised her lips to press a kiss against his before gazing at him with tears in her eyes. A soft moan escaped her when he thrust deeply into her and paused.

"I can feel you, too," she whispered. "I want you, Saber. All of you."

Saber lowered his body over hers and began thrusting harder. His jaw clenched tightly to prevent himself from marking her. He wanted to so badly. She would always be his in his heart. There was no way he could ever have another woman. In his heart, Taylor had been his *Amate* from the first day he had held her in his arms.

Pressing his lips against the curve of her shoulder, he thrust once more before releasing a low groan as she came apart in his arms. His eyes closed when she locked down on him, holding him to her as she pulsed around his thick shaft. The slender thread on his self-control snapped and he shook with the force of his release.

You are my Amate, he thought desperately, holding her tightly against his body as he pumped his seed deep into her womb. *In my heart, I have claimed you.*

Chapter 9

"Saber?" Taylor called out groggily the next morning.

She reached out her hand to touch Saber's side of the bed. Rolling to her side, she ran her hand over his pillow, a smile curving her lips. He had been – incredible. It was the only word that she could think of to describe their night together.

Sitting up, she looked around the room. She grinned at the tenderness that she felt. It was just added proof that last night hadn't been a dream.

"Or rather, another hopeful one," she muttered as she slid out of the bed. "It was a wonderful dream come true."

She walked around the bed and stepped into the bathroom. Taking a quick shower, she wrapped a thick towel around her before stepping out of the room to retrieve the fresh change of clothes that she had brought with her. Spying her backpack, she picked it up and set it on the couch.

She pulled out a dark green pullover, jeans, panties, and the bra that she hadn't bothered to wear last night. Glancing up, she saw Saber out in the garden. Sweat glistened on his body. He was only wearing a pair of long, jogging pants. He was moving in the familiar pattern she saw him, Hunter, and the other warriors doing during their training.

His arms moved in a beautiful, fluid motion. He had built up his upper muscle strength since his injury.

The year he had been confined to a wheelchair was probably the reason. He held a long pole in his left hand and was twirling it above his head. Her hand flew to her mouth to keep the cry from escaping when she saw him turn. His bad leg gave out on him, causing him to stumble. The only thing that kept him from falling was the pole in his hand.

She saw his hand tighten on it until his knuckles shone white with his frustration. After a few moments, he straightened and tried the move again. Each time, his leg gave out on him, causing him to stumble. Her heart skipped with each move.

Tears glistened in her eyes when he tried a different move. He staggered, this time unable to catch himself. He twisted as he fell, landing on the ground where he lay staring up at the early morning sky.

Taylor dropped the clothes in her hand and walked slowly through the opened doors. Padding on bare feet, he didn't hear her until she was just a few feet away from him. His head turned and their eyes locked. His were filled with anger, frustration and… regret. She knew hers were filled with tears. She hurt for him, with him.

He rolled, grabbing the pole. She watched as he struggled to his feet. Something warned her not to help. Perhaps it was the rigidness in his shoulders or the tension in the air, but either way, it told her that he wasn't in a good place right now.

She waited patiently for him to straighten. Swallowing, panic began to build inside her when he wouldn't look at her. Taking a step closer to him, she hesitated when he jerked backwards, stumbling again.

"Don't," she whispered, reaching her hand out to him. "Don't, Saber. Please… Don't shut me out."

Saber turned to look at her then. Taylor shook her head, tears pooling in her eyes before spilling down her cheeks. The distant look in his eyes and the silence told her what he was doing. He wasn't just closing her out… He was letting her go.

"No," she sobbed, her hand clenching and falling to her side. "You love me. I know you do. I'm your *Amate*. I belong to you. Last night…."

"Stop!" His sharp order ricocheted through her.

Taylor shook her head. "You love me," she insisted.

"I need you to leave," he said, looking away from her for a moment before he turned back to gaze down at her with blazing eyes filled with pain. "I want you to leave, and not come back this time, Taylor."

"NO!" She cried in frustration, stepping toward him. "I belong to you! You are mine! You are my *Amate*. I claimed you last night," she insisted, stepping up in front of him and dropping the towel. "I gave myself to you, Saber. I gave you more than my body. I gave you my heart," she whispered, tilting her head to look up at him with desperate eyes.

His hand rose. For a moment, she thought he would admit that he was wrong, but instead, his fingers wrapped around her wrist and he lifted it between them. He shook his head as he stared down at her. Her lips trembled at the harsh coldness that clouded his eyes.

"You do not wear my claim upon your wrist, just as I do not wear yours," he said, releasing her wrist as if the touch of her skin burned him. "And we never will."

Taylor watched in disbelief as he awkwardly bent down and picked up the towel that she had dropped. He carefully wrapped it around her, before using the pole to step back. She turned her gaze away from him when he looked back at her with a blank expression.

"Tell me," she whispered, looking back at him once again. "Tell me that you don't love me, Saber. Tell me that you don't love me and that you want me to leave and not come back, but look me in the eye when you say it."

Taylor braced herself for the wave of pain that she knew was about to hit her. He was going to do it. She could see the resignation in his eyes. He was going to let her go, whether she wanted to go or not.

"I don't love you, Taylor. I want you to leave and not come back," Saber said in a quiet voice, never breaking eye contact with her.

The pain was worse than she ever imagined it could be. It felt as if someone was ripping her heart out of her chest. Swallowing, she tilted her head, but didn't scream.

"You're a terrible liar, Saber," Taylor whispered, staring back at him before she lowered her head, letting her hair fall forward to conceal the fresh tears running down her face. "I'll leave, but there is something you need to know," she said, looking up again. "I love you. I have from the moment I met you.

I'm going to go away for a while. There is an aid mission that I was asked to go on. I wasn't going to go because...." She paused, clamping her lips together to get control of her composure before continuing. "I'm giving you three months to think over whether you really want me out of your life. When I return, I'll come by one last time. If you want me, place a yellow ribbon on the tree in the front courtyard. If I don't see it, you'll never see me again. I won't chase you, Saber. I love you for you, not your body. I love the man inside, but I need him to love me, too."

Turning on her heel, she walked back into the house. Dropping the towel, she pulled on her shirt and pants and slipped on her shoes. Grabbing her bra and panties, she stuffed them back into her backpack. Picking it up, she walked out of the house without a backwards glance. She didn't want him to see the utter grief that was tearing her apart.

..*

Saber watched as Taylor walked back into the house. From where he was standing, he could see her getting dressed. His fingers gripped the pole in his hands until he felt sure that it would crumble under the pressure of his grasp.

His eyes burned when she turned and walked out of the house without a backwards look. Shaking, he heard the sound of her transport as it started. A moment later, it flew over his house, heading back in the direction of Hunter and Jesse's house. It was only when she was out of sight that he gave in to the grief. A loud gasp escaped him as he sank back down to the ground. The pole clattered against the tile and he leaned forward, rocking as pain exploded through him.

Sitting back, he tilted his head back and roared in rage. His body shook with the force of his pain. It was far worse than what the doctors had told him yesterday.

"You are lucky to still have your leg," the surgeon had told him. "There is nothing else we can do. The damage was too great even for the bone regenerator to repair. The nerve damage is irreversible. I had to remove almost an inch of fragmented bone during this last surgery. Your body is rejecting the bone graft that was done. I've injected a new anti-rejection agent in the hopes that we can still save it. If the graft holds long enough for the new bone to have a chance to fuse, then you should be fine. If this doesn't work, it will be necessary to amputate your leg."

Saber's eyes burned as he looked up at the sky. In his mind's eye, all he could see was Taylor's beautiful face as he made love to her. He didn't know how it was possible for a male to survive such agony. For the first time in his life, he understood the bond between a Trivator and his *Amate*.

"Goddess, help me," he whispered. "I love her so much. Help me."

Chapter 10

"Taylor, are you sure about this?" Jesse asked, following her sister as she picked up another item and tossed it into her backpack. "What happened last night? Taylor," Jesse reached out and touched Taylor's arm when she tried to walk around her again. "Talk to me. I'm here for you. I always have been."

Taylor stopped, her hands twisting the shirt she had grabbed. She stared at the wall before she released the breath she was holding. Turning, she sank down on the edge of the bed, her head bowed.

"I have to go away for a little while, Jesse," she whispered. "I need… I need to find myself."

Jesse's eyes softened at the confusion in Taylor's voice. Kneeling on the floor in front of her sister, Jesse laid her hands over Taylor's trembling ones. A tear drop landed on the back of her hand. Concern swept through Jesse. Taylor had always been the bubbly one of the three sisters. Seeing her in so much pain and not being able to do anything about it was tearing Jesse apart.

"What did Saber do to you?" Jesse asked.

Taylor swallowed before she looked at Jesse. Her eyes were full of unshed tears. She pulled one hand free and wiped angrily at her cheek when they spilled over.

"He lied to me," Taylor whispered. "He said he wanted me to leave and not come back. He said he didn't love me."

Jesse shook her head and cupped Taylor's cheek. "He adores you," she said in a firm voice. "He's just going through a rough time."

"Five years, Jesse," Taylor said, sliding off the bed and stepping around her older sister. Wrapping her arms around her waist, she turned to look at Jesse. "It's been almost five years since the mission and his return. I've tried to be patient. I went into physical therapy to help him, but he fights me. He… He's changed so much, but I still love him. It hurts, Jesse. It hurts so much and I don't know how to make it stop."

Jesse rose to her feet and wrapped her arms around Taylor's trembling body. She didn't say anything. She closed her eyes and wished there was a magic answer to ease the pain Taylor was feeling.

"So, where are you going?" She asked, pulling back.

Taylor sniffed and pulled away. "There is a practicum that I was offered to finish out my studies early. It is an aid mission to the Dises V star system. They haven't been in the Alliance for very long. I… I wasn't going to go. I could finish my degree here, but this is a chance to finish early and really apply what I've been learning."

"Taylor…," Jesse whispered, her hand going to her throat. "How long will you be gone? Who is going? When are you leaving?"

Taylor stuffed the shirt she was holding into the backpack she always carried. "Three months. There are six of us from my class going. The transport is leaving this afternoon. I've got to hurry if I'm going to make it."

"Oh, Taylor, surely there is another way," Jesse said, twisting her hands together.

Taylor turned and looked at Jesse's worried face. Stepping up, she gave her big sister a tight hug before stepping back. Shaking her head, she opened the drawer next to the bed and pulled out a picture of her, Jesse, Jordan, and their dad. Staring at it, she slid it into the front pocket of her backpack.

"I've grown up, Jesse," she said in a firm voice. "You, Jordan, and Dad, you've all done a great job, but it's time for me to find out who I am. I love you. I don't think I tell you that enough, or thank you for everything you've done."

"You never have to thank me, Taylor," Jesse protested. "You are family."

Taylor zipped her bag closed and slung it over her shoulder. "I know," she said. "Will you tell Jordan goodbye for me?"

Jesse pressed her lips together so she wouldn't cry and nodded. Taylor could see this was difficult for Jesse. For the moment at least, a sense of calm came over her. This would give both her and Saber time to see if they really were meant to go their separate ways.

"I love you, Taylor," Jesse said in a quivering voice. "I expect to hear from you at least once a week. Remember to be careful."

Taylor chuckled. "I'm too fast for a bunch of old fuddy-duddies to catch me," she teased to cover her own feelings. "I need to give Leila and Lyon a kiss before I go. I'm going to miss those two."

Jesse laughed and shook her head. "Shana and Scout are going to be furious that they aren't here to see you off!" She warned, slipping her arm through Taylor's.

Taylor smiled. "Kali and Razor needed them to babysit while they went on that diplomatic mission," she said. "Kali taught me a few of her moves. She is really cool on the obstacle course down at the training center. She ran circles around the young recruits."

"I know," Jesse replied with a sigh, running her hand over her slightly plumper figure. "I might have been able to keep up with her before the kids."

Taylor squeezed Jesse's arm. "And Hunter," she teased. "Admit it. He loves feeding you and he can't keep his hands off you."

Jesse blushed and grinned. "He likes that I'm slightly curvier," she admitted, before she drew in a deep breath. "Just promise me that you'll be safe."

"Always," Taylor replied, bending to kiss Lyon before picking up Leila and hugging her. "I'll miss you, sweet pea."

Leila giggled, looking at Jesse and holding out her arms. "Mama," she squealed.

Jesse looked at Charma, their housekeeper. "Can you watch these two for just a bit longer?" She asked.

"Of course, Jesse," Charma said, clapping her hands for Leila. "I think it is time to go swimming."

"Yay!" Lyon shouted, jumping to his feet and taking off out the door to the garden.

"I'll be there in just a few minutes," Jesse promised.

Charma nodded, turning to hurry after Lyon. "Take your time," she said, stepping out of the door and calling for Lyon to wait up for her.

Taylor chuckled and turned toward the front door. She could hear the sound of a transport out front. Buzz, one of her classmates, was picking her up.

"My ride's here," Taylor said in a thick voice. "If Saber tries to contact me… Just let him know I think it is best if we don't talk to each other for a while. I want him to know I meant what I said."

Jesse frowned. "What did you tell him?" She asked in concern.

Taylor paused at the front door and gave Jesse a weak smile. "That if he didn't get his shit together by the time I get back, that I'm moving on with my life. I can't do this anymore, Jesse. I love him too much to watch him destroy what we have because he can't accept that I don't need a warrior as an Amate, I need the man."

Jesse nodded and hugged Taylor again. "He'll realize that," she promised. "If he doesn't, Hunter and Dagger will whip his ass."

Taylor laughed and opened the door. "Maybe that is what he needs," she teased. "I'll see you in a few months."

"Be safe," Jesse called out, watching Taylor jog over to the transport.

Taylor had grown up. Jesse waved again as the transport lifted off the ground. A sad smile curved her lips. Saber better get his shit together or he was going to lose the best thing that ever happened to him.

..*

Saber grimaced when he heard the banging on his front door. He laid his head back on the couch when it stopped and closed his eyes again. For a moment, he wondered if he had imagined it, as his head was still making the loud pounding that had woken him from a fitful sleep.

He jerked when he felt the presence of someone else in the room. His hand groped for the weapon he usually carried; instead, his fingers wrapped around his cane. Swinging it upward, he grunted.

"What do you think you are doing?" Hunter demanded, glaring down at where Saber was sprawled on the couch.

"That's the problem, he isn't thinking – as usual," Dagger added, giving the voice command for the panels in the ceiling to change to clear.

"*Shewta*! What are you two doing here? I know I locked the door," Saber muttered, releasing the cane that Hunter was holding and covering his eyes. "Shut out the light," he demanded in a thick, slightly slurred voice.

"No," Dagger said, walking over to sit down in the chair across from Saber.

"Sunshade mode," Saber hissed, breathing a sigh when the panels darkened to block part of the sun, but not all of it. Pushing up into a sitting position, he leaned forward and drew in a deep breath, hoping that the room would stop spinning. "What are you doing here?"

"Trying not to kill your ass," Hunter snapped in irritation. "You made Jesse cry!"

Saber glanced up at Hunter's angry face and grimaced. He knew what was about to happen. It had been building for the past five years. With a weary sigh, he leaned back and stared at Hunter, ignoring the pounding in his head from too much liquor.

"Taylor…," Saber started to say before he clamped his lips shut at the dark scowl on Hunter's face.

"Gone," Hunter snapped again, moving to sit down in the other chair across from Saber. "She left yesterday afternoon on an aid mission to Dises V."

Saber groaned and leaned back, running his hand over his hair as he stared up at the shadowed sky. Dises V had only been in the Alliance for the last six months.

"As you know, the Eastern sector on Dises V reached out and requested help from the Alliance. The council agreed to provide limited support and medical aid. The problem is tensions have been mounting over the last couple of months between the two ruling sectors. The Eastern sector is embracing the Alliance while the Western opposes it. The Western argues that the Alliance has no jurisdiction to be on the planet. They have been using the inhabitants of the Eastern regions to supply their labor force. The Eastern sector is smaller and has been the main source of that labor over the last few centuries. They want to conform to Alliance standards and free all those sold into servitude. Razor is trying to negotiate a peace accord and set up trade to help the Eastern regions receive additional resources to make the transition easier," Hunter bluntly informed Saber.

"What Razor really wants to do is flatten the Western sectors refusing to comply, but there are too many innocents being held hostage by the rebel groups in the Western regions," Dagger added, bending forward to pick up Saber's cane and twirling it between his fingers. "If you ask me, the whole region is about to explode."

"Razor has requested additional troops, but the council is hoping to avoid that. They believe if the Eastern region is aware that more troops are on their way, things will escalate before a treaty can be signed. The Western region insists that they deal with their people. That this is a matter between them, not the Alliance."

Saber scowled at Hunter. "That makes absolutely no sense. If the council knows how dangerous the situation is, why don't they agree with Razor's demands? You would think they would realize that he understands the situation and wouldn't request additional troops unless he suspected something was about to happen. Surely, the ruling faction of the Western region knows better than to oppose Razor?"

He muttered. "Why would you allow Taylor to go to that region knowing it is about to explode?"

Hunter's eyes narrowed. "I didn't," he bit out. "She left while I was in a closed meeting. Jesse feels Taylor is old enough to make her own decisions."

Saber grimaced and glared at Dagger, holding his hand out. Dagger tossed the cane he had been playing with to Saber. Leaning heavily on it, Saber struggled to a standing position.

"Call her back," Saber grunted. "This isn't Earth. Jesse should know that Taylor is under your protection. There is no 'old' enough. The duty of a Trivator demands that he care for the females under his protection until that protection is passed to another."

"You should have thought about that before you hurt her, Saber," Hunter said in a cold, hard voice. "I gave my trust to you that you would protect Taylor."

"I...," Saber started to say before he pressed his lips together and turned away. Walking stiffly, he leaned on the cane for support. "It is better that you don't trust me. It is time for you to leave," he said in a quiet voice.

"No."

Saber turned in surprise upon hearing the determination in both Hunter's and Dagger's voices when they said the word at the same time. He stared warily at the two men as they rose. Hunter crossed his arms while Dagger stood across from him, his fingers moving restlessly by his side.

"You've wallowed in your self-pity long enough," Dagger replied with a humorless, sharp-tooth grin. "We've decided we want the old Saber back."

"I didn't mind too much before because it gave Taylor time to grow up," Hunter replied with a shrug. "The problem is, she is grown up now. I know that Taylor spent the night with you before she left," he continued. "Did you claim her?"

Saber flushed and looked away. "Do you think I don't realize that she is grown?" He asked in a thick voice.

"That's not what I asked," Hunter growled in a low tone. "I asked if you claimed Taylor the other night, Saber."

Saber turned and glared at Hunter, refusing to answer his question. What could he say? Yes, he took Taylor, but cast her aside the next morning. The flush on his face deepened with shame and remorse. That was exactly what he had done. He had used her as if she was a....

"She deserves more than a broken warrior," he muttered, sinking back down onto the couch.

His head jerked up when both Hunter and Dagger burst out into bitter laughter. He glared at them. His head was about to explode, his throat felt like he had swallowed a handful of sand, and his heart felt like he had ripped it out of his chest, and the two men he considered his brothers thought it was funny.

"I don't see what is so humorous in the situation," he growled, glancing back and forth at them.

"Broken?" Dagger said with a shake of his head. "I spent two years in a fucking fight ring. You want to talk about broken...." He drew in a hissing breath and stared at Saber with dark, piercing eyes. "I still have nightmares. If it wasn't for Jordan...." His voice died and he shook his head again. "Don't you fucking talk to me about being broken."

Saber glanced at Hunter's calm face. "He's right," Hunter said. "I was there with you when you were wounded, Saber. You weren't the only one hurt. I had to learn to walk again, too. If not for the nano-charges implanted in my spine, I wouldn't even be able to stand up."

A wave of shame flashed through Saber. They were right. Dagger's two years of captivity had left their own deep scars, both inside and out. If not for Jordan Sampson, his friend would have died in one of those illegal rings and no one would have been the wiser. They had all accepted that he had been killed when the fighter he was flying exploded shortly after crashing.

If not for Hunter, Saber would have been dead as well. The attack on them was strangely reminiscent of what was happening on Dises V. The thought of Taylor caught up in a civil uprising filled Saber with rage.

A soft moan escaped Saber when he bowed his head. Reaching up, he rubbed his throbbing brow. For the first time in his life, he wasn't sure what to do.

"The healer said if this latest procedure on my leg doesn't work, they may have to amputate it," he finally said in a rough voice.

"If it happens, you deal with it. Do you really think that Taylor would turn you away because of it?" Hunter asked, sitting back down in the chair across from Saber and staring at him. "Taylor, Jordan, and Jesse are different. Taylor spent the last five years studying ways to help you, Saber. What Trivator female do you know would have done that?"

"None," Saber reluctantly admitted as he turned to watch as Dagger walked over to the set of doors.

Saber studied the stiff shoulders of his friend. He knew that Dagger was remembering the dark times in his own life. After several long seconds, Dagger turned and looked at him.

"What Trivator female do you know would spend two years searching for a dead warrior, then when she found him, refuse to leave him behind, no matter how dangerous it was to her own life? Jordan came close to dying, more than once," Dagger said in a gruff voice. "If not for her… I thought I was going insane. She brought me back, as much as I could be," he admitted, looking away.

"You are right," Saber finally admitted with a tired sigh. "Taylor's last words to me were that she loved me, and that I was lying to her. She was right. I do love her." He turned his head back to Hunter and rose stiffly again. "Hunter, I would like to request your permission to claim Taylor as my *Amate*. I swear I will do everything in my power to protect her," Saber said in a solemn voice.

Hunter rose and looked at Saber with a crooked grin. Saber knew what he would see, and it wasn't impressive. His clothes were wrinkled. He smelled of liquor, and he desperately needed a shower. Straightening his shoulders, he stared back at Hunter with determination.

"I accept your request," Hunter said with a smile. "Now, you just have to get Jesse to agree. She isn't very happy with you at the moment."

Dagger stepped up and slapped Saber on the shoulder, chuckling when Saber winced and shot him a nasty glare. He knew Dagger had done it on purpose. Dagger was probably wishing he had slapped him upside the head.

"Neither is Jordan," Dagger grinned.

Saber nodded with a wry grin. "The one who is the most angry with me at the moment is Taylor," he replied. "I need to get cleaned up. I don't want her to see me this way, though it is no less than I deserve."

Hunter shook his head. "She told Jesse she didn't want to see or hear from you until she returned. Jesse said Taylor was quite adamant about it," he said with a grimace.

Saber swallowed. *That isn't going to happen. She is going to talk to me even if it means getting on the next transport to Dises V to do it!*

"How long did she say she was going to be gone again?" Saber asked, looking at Hunter's slightly amused expression with dread.

"Three months," Hunter replied. "You have three months to get yourself together."

Another groan escaped Saber. He would still contact Taylor. She might not want to see or talk to him, but he had a lot to say to her. Each sentence began with the phrase 'I'm such a moron'.

Chapter 11

Dises V: Two months later.

"Taylor, over here!" Buzz called from the other side of the large tent.

"Be right there!" Taylor hollered back, smiling down at the little boy that she had helped. "Remember to do your exercises every day. Before you know it, you'll be able to play just like the other boys."

"I will," the boy said, staring up at Taylor with a touch of hero worship.

Standing, Taylor smiled at the boy's mother, Karna. She had brought him in with a compound fractured arm almost three weeks ago. It had taken two surgeries for the healers to repair all the damage.

"Thank you, PT Taylor," Karna said with a nervous smile. "You are different from the other warriors. I am glad my son was given into your care."

Londius, or Lonnie as Taylor had nicknamed him, slid off the table and wrapped his arms around her waist. She hugged him back and ruffled his hair. At seven, he was full of energy and reminded her of herself when she was that age.

"It's just Taylor, and I am glad too," Taylor said with a slightly worried smile. "I hope you have a safe trip home. I thought I heard the sound of explosions earlier.

Karna nodded. "Yes, the unrest is growing. I hope that the two sides come to terms soon. For the Western to want to use people the way they do...." She paused and shook her head. "It is wrong, but there are more of them than there are here in the Eastern region."

"I agree," Taylor replied, turning when Buzz called to her again. "I have to go. Don't forget your exercises, Lonnie."

"Goodbye, PT Taylor," Lonnie called, skipping ahead of his mother.

Taylor grinned before turning. She had only taken two steps when the communicator at her waist buzzed. Pulling it free from the clip, she glanced down at the message. A choked giggle escaped her.

"What's so funny?" Buzz asked, looking at the screen before he raised an eyebrow at her. "What kind of a warrior sends a female pictures of yellow pieces of cloth?"

Taylor hugged the communicator to her chest and scowled at her best friend. "One that knows he is on my shit list," she replied, sticking her tongue out at Buzz. "What did you need?"

Buzz frowned and shook his head at her. "I don't understand what you see in that male. He is old. I am closer to your age and I am whole," he grumbled.

"There's nothing wrong with Saber!" Taylor said sharply, glaring in warning at Buzz. "Where did that come from, anyway? We're best buds, not – you know – like interested in each other."

Buzz turned unexpectedly. Taylor stared up at him in surprise when he reached out and tightly gripped her arms between his hands. Tilting her head to the side to look up at him, she realized that he had really gone through a growing spurt over the last two years.

"Best buds," he muttered, staring down at her in frustration. "This is a term you used when we first met. You said it meant friends. That was fine for when we were younger, but I have been waiting for you to reach the age of acceptance."

"Age of acceptance," Taylor mumbled, trying to understand what the hell was going on. "That is like so – retro. I mean, back on my planet, I think they stopped talking like that about a hundred years ago."

"You are not on your planet, Taylor," Buzz bit out harshly. "You are on mine!"

Taylor looked around the tented clinic that had been set up. "Technically, we aren't on either," she said with a confused smile.

"I know that," Buzz growled. "That's not the point! The point is…."

Buzz's words were cut short by a loud explosion that shook the tent. His arms immediately wrapped around Taylor and he turned to cover her as part of the tent collapsed. The sound of sirens and additional explosions shook the ground.

"We've got to get out of here," Buzz said in a low, urgent voice, holding onto Taylor.

Taylor nodded, slipping her hand into his and squeezing it. In the background, she could hear yelling and the sounds of fighter transports flying overhead. Another series of explosions rattled the tent. They barely made it out the other side when the force of a missile striking it sent them both flying through the air.

A scream tore from Taylor's throat as she hit the ground and rolled. The force of the impact knocked the breath out of her and her ears were ringing from the thunderous sound. Crawling, she rolled under a large trailer used to haul material behind a ground cruiser.

More missiles struck close by, destroying many of the new medical buildings. Through a cloud of smoke, Taylor saw Lonnie's familiar form on the other side of the gate. He was sitting on the ground between two buildings, crying.

Rolling out from under the trailer, Taylor stumbled to her feet. She covered her nose and mouth with her arm to keep from breathing in the smoke from the fires caused by the explosions.

Her eyes swept the area. She didn't see Buzz anywhere. Shaking her head, she tried to clear the ringing in her ears as she stumbled through the debris. She ignored the men that ran by her, shouting; her only thought was to reach the little boy.

She gasped when a hand suddenly reached out and grabbed her arm. Turning, she started to strike out when she saw Buzz's dirty face gazing at her. Turning, she threw her arms around his neck in a brief hug.

"We've got to go," he shouted, pointing in the opposite direction.

"No!" Taylor cried out, trying to break his grip and pointing to where she had been going. "Lonnie!"

Buzz turned and looked in the direction that Taylor was pointing. A grim expression crossed his face. Nodding to Taylor, he turned and started running toward the little boy.

Taylor ran beside him, glancing with fear as several Trivator warriors raised their weapons and began firing in the direction they were going. Fear for the little boy gave her an adrenaline rush and she sprinted past Buzz when he stumbled as the ground shook under their feet again.

"Lonnie," Taylor cried out, kneeling in front of the boy. "Are you hurt? Where is your mom?"

Lonnie shook his head, looking wildly around him. "I don't know," he choked out. "There was an explosion and we were running and I lost her. I didn't know what to do. I thought she might come back to the tent."

"Taylor, we've got to get out of here," Buzz said, scooping the boy up in his arms.

Taylor nodded. She rose and started to turn when she heard the sound of a cry. In the narrow alley, Taylor spotted Karna. She was struggling to climb over some fallen debris.

"Take him to one of the transports," Taylor instructed. "I'll help his mother."

"Taylor," Buzz started to argue.

Taylor shook her head and started to move away from Buzz. "I can't carry him, Buzz, you'll have to do it. Go!" She ordered, turning and running down the alley.

Taylor glanced over her shoulder in time to see Buzz jerk as another blast hit close. He shot her a frustrated look before turning on his heel and running back to the compound. Taylor didn't wait any longer.

"Here, let me help," she said, rushing up to where Karna was struggling.

"Londius?" Karna asked as she turned and looked at Taylor with frightened eyes.

"Buzz has him," Taylor said, wincing at the sounds of the fighting drawing nearer.

"My skirt is caught," Karna said, jerking at the back of her skirt.

Taylor grabbed a handful of the material and pulled. The sound of tearing could barely be heard over the shouts of the warriors, the blasts, and the overhead fighter transports attacking the invading forces.

"You're free! This way," Taylor said, grabbing Karna's hand and pulling her forward.

Taylor stopped at the end of the alley and glanced around the corner. She could see a group of Trivator warriors moving down along the sides of the buildings. They were returning fire on the rebels.

Her head jerked up when a fighter moved slowly over the area, striking with a frightening precision into several buildings further down the road. Squeezing Karna's hand, Taylor drew in a deep breath and took off running. The right side of the gate that led into the compound lay on the ground. The other gate hung crooked, bent from flying debris.

"There's Buzz; go to him! He knows where Lonnie is," Taylor called out, turning toward the area where she saw a wounded soldier fall.

Taylor's heart pounded as she ran to the man. He was holding his side, but she could see blood coming from his leg as well. Falling to her knees, she pulled the scarf holding her hair back from her head and untied it.

"How bad is your side?" She asked breathlessly, tying the scarf around his thigh to stem the blood long enough for her to check his side.

"Run, female!" The warrior growled with a furious look. "You should not be here."

Taylor sent him a shaky grin. "I don't think any of us should be here," she replied, throwing herself over him when a series of rapid fire struck the building to the left of them. "Can you get up?"

"Yes," the warrior hissed, struggling up with Taylor's help. "Who are you?"

"Taylor Sampson," she replied, wrapping her arm around his waist. "Come on."

The warrior grimly nodded. Taylor saw him turn pale, but he didn't complain. She could tell he had more wounds than she had seen at first. He had blood coming from his shoulder and a gash along his forehead.

"What's happening?" Taylor asked as they struggled across the compound, pausing briefly to wait for the gunfire to clear before moving to the next area of cover.

"Talks have broken down," the man grunted. "The West has declared a separation from the Alliance and has identified the Eastern region as part of their territory. The planet is on the verge of a Civil War. The Eastern side is rebelling. They hope the Alliance will send in troops to support them. The Western council that was working with Razor has been assassinated and a new governing board of extremists has taken over."

Taylor paled. The little that she knew of the situation, the Western had been on the verge of accepting an agreement. She knew that Razor was there working on the negotiations.

She stumbled when his leg gave out under him. He was losing a lot more blood than she'd realized. Relief washed through her when two of the military medics rushed forward and grabbed him. She stepped back and realized that she was near the tent where she and Buzz had been working.

"Prepare for evacuation one!" One of the medics called out. "We have been told to pull back to the military base."

Taylor nodded. Her eyes swept over the compound. It was just a temporary medical station, not a military one. She swallowed as she saw more injured soldiers being transported in and additional support coverage converging in the center.

She started forward before she remembered her backpack. Turning, she hurried back to the living quarters. She saw several people running out. Pushing past them, she ran up the stairs. She was almost to the third floor when she heard her name.

"Taylor," Buzz called out from the second floor landing. "We have been ordered to evacuate."

Taylor looked down over the railing. "I know. I'm just grabbing my backpack," she replied.

Buzz nodded. "Hurry. I'll wait for you," he said with a worried glance down the stairwell.

Taylor nodded and hurried up the last few steps. Holding onto the wall when the building shook, she jogged down the corridor to her room. She pushed the door open and stepped inside. It didn't take her long to pack the few things she had brought.

Her eyes froze on the two pictures next to the bed. One was of her, Jesse, Jordan, and their dad. The other was a picture of her and Saber that Jordan had taken a few months ago on her birthday. They had been sitting outside watching Lyon and Leila. She was holding Leila while Lyon was climbing on Saber's back. She had leaned in to nibble on Lyon's fingers. Saber had turned his head to watch and she had surprised him with a kiss.

Her fingers trembled as she grabbed the pictures off the side table. Stuffing them in her backpack, she quickly zipped it closed and slid the straps over her shoulders. She had just opened the door when the world around her exploded.

Chapter 12

Saber lifted the weights before slowly lowering them back down. He had gone in for a follow up with the healer today. He looked at his right leg and grinned. It would never be perfect, but over the last two months a lot had changed.

He rubbed his leg through the new biotech brace and swallowed. The new medication had worked. The synthetic bone they had implanted in his leg had finally fused with the natural bone. The rejection inhibitors had kept his body from rejecting it. He would need to have regular injections, probably for the rest of his life, but it was a small price to pay. On top of that, he had been given an experimental brace the university was developing.

"Taylor," Saber whispered, fingering the material.

He closed his eyes as a shaft of pain swept through him. She had been behind it all. She was the reason the Medical Research department had contacted him. Her degree was in Physical Therapy and Developmental Research. She had been working in the Biotech labs researching a new material using the same nanotechnology that had been implanted into Hunter.

Swinging around, he stood up. The nagging pain from the unhealed bone was finally gone. He could still feel the stiffness in his leg, but he was slowly working it out. The damaged nerves were no longer an issue as long as he had the brace on. A monitor detected his movements and sent small electrical impulses into the brace, causing his leg to react in a natural, fluid movement.

Stretching, he bent and picked up a towel to wipe the sweat from his face. He frowned when he saw the shadow of a transport fly over the house. He raised his hand to show Hunter that he saw him.

He walked across the nearly completed garden. Taking the steps two at a time, a wave of pleasure swept through him. He would never take the simple movement of walking for granted again.

Opening the door, he waited as Dagger and Hunter both slid out of the transport. His smile faded when he saw the tense look on their faces. It was the same look that they wore before some of their more dangerous missions.

"What happened?" Saber asked, stiffening when he saw the anger burning in Hunter's eyes.

"Let's go inside," Hunter said with a nod.

Saber stood aside as both men entered. He followed them into the living room and turned to face them. He tossed the towel onto the low table and folded his arms across his chest.

"How is your leg?" Hunter asked in a taut voice.

"Good, why?" Saber responded, looking between the two men. Dagger's eyes narrowed on the brace Saber was wearing. "Prototype. It does something similar to the implant Hunter has."

"Can you fight?" Dagger asked with an intense stare.

Saber raised an eyebrow and looked back at Hunter who nodded. His stomach tightened when he saw something savage burning in Hunter's eyes. It was the same look that he had when Jesse, Jordan, and Taylor had been surrounded by the human males who planned to rape and kill them.

"Is she alive?" He asked in a quiet voice.

"Yes," Hunter replied in a clipped tone. "What I'm about to tell you has not been authorized by the Lead Council."

"What we are going to do has not been authorized either… except by Razor," Dagger added with a savage grin.

"Two days ago, militants killed the ruling Western Council on Dises V. They broke off negotiations and attacked the city of Drues," Hunter explained.

"Drues," Saber muttered, raising his hand and running it down over his face. "Isn't that where Taylor's medical group is stationed?"

"Yes," Hunter said with a tired sigh. "It was an unexpected move. The city is one of the largest in the Eastern sector, but it is also one of the furthest from the Western border."

"You said she is alive," Saber replied, dropping his hand to his side. "Surely, the forces there evacuated the medical staff, especially knowing it was made up of volunteers."

Hunter nodded. "Yes, they were evacuated, but Taylor didn't make it. One of the students said he was waiting for her to grab her backpack when the barracks was hit. He was pulled out, but the rescue team didn't realize that Taylor was still in there."

Saber swallowed and glanced down at his clenched fists. If he lost her… He looked up at Hunter. There was more. She had to make it. He had said that she wasn't dead.

"Where is she?" He asked in a harsh voice.

Hunter glanced at Dagger. Dagger walked over to the vidcom and slid a chip into it. Saber stepped closer. He recognized Taylor immediately. She was sitting in a chair. There was dried blood on her face and she looked extremely young and pale. He couldn't see her eyes because they were covered, but he could see her lips moving.

"This was sent to Razor," Hunter said in a grim tone. "The militant group that took over the Western government recognized Taylor and is using her to keep Razor from flattening the entire region. They said she will be tried as a traitor and kept at an undisclosed location until her execution."

Saber stepped closer, watching Taylor's lips. His hand rose to touch her face. He could see the bruising along her cheek under the cloth wrapped around her eyes. His eyes moved down to her lips again and a fierce wave of fire seared him.

I love you, Saber. I love you, Saber.

He could see what she was saying. She was telling him goodbye in her own way. Turning, he stared at Hunter and Dagger.

"When do we leave?" He asked.

"Tonight," Hunter said. "Razor will brief us when we get there. No one else but us and two others know about this mission."

***

Later that evening, Saber stood on the remote landing field that was used for training. He had packed his gear carefully, going for what he thought would be the most essential in a retrieval mission. Taylor's bloody and bruised face haunted him as he prepared. Her silent words sent a wave of deadly calm and purpose through him. He would get her back, and he would kill anyone who tried to stop him.

He stood silently on the dark field as an advance attack transport appeared over the treetops. Whoever was handling it knew what they were doing. They were coming in fast and dark. A moment later, the ship landed on the tarmac and the rear platform lowered to reveal a soft, dim red light. Saber watched as three men stepped out onto the platform and waited for them.

"Sword, Thunder, and Trig will be our support team," Hunter said, nodding to the three men as they strode forward.

"I'm surprised you're still alive," Saber said, nodding at Dagger's older brother, Trig, as he walked by him. "I expected Dagger to kill your ass the next time he saw you."

Trig glanced at Dagger and grinned. "He still threatens to, but Jordan won't let him. She likes me," he boasted before his smile died. "This would tear both

Jordan and Hunter's mates up if they knew what was happening."

Saber nodded, stepping inside behind Thunder, Sword, Hunter, and Dagger. He watched as Hunter and Dagger secured their weapons under the seat.

"Yes, but knowing those two, they would be going in after Taylor, if they did," he said, wrapping his hand around the hold bar above the seats as Thunder lifted off the tarmac.

Trig glanced at Saber's leg. "I heard you were wounded pretty badly," he said, doubt clouding his expression. "Are you fit for the mission?"

Saber heard the reservation in Trig's voice. He reacted with a swift, decisive move. His hand released the hold bar and he grabbed Trig's arm and twisted. Using his bad leg, he kicked Trig's feet out from under him. Within seconds, he had Trig on his stomach with his arm bent at an awkward angle. He could feel the other men's eyes on him as he held Trig down on the metal floor of the ship, the knife that he carried pressed to the man's throat.

Saber could feel the adrenaline rushing through his system. "What do you think?" He asked in a deadly voice.

Trig winced when the knife pierced his skin. "I think you've put on some muscle since I last saw you. What the hell have you been doing?" He muttered.

Tense laughter echoed through the ship as Saber stepped back. He reached down and helped Trig back to his feet. Sheathing the knife at his waist, he looked up when Trig touched his neck.

"You know, a simple yes would have worked just as well," Trig complained, pulling a cloth from his shirt and holding it against his neck.

Saber glanced away and shrugged. "I could have," he said, looking back at Trig with an intense stare. "But, you would have doubted it. This mission is too important to worry whether one of us on the team is fit for duty."

Trig grimaced. "True," he muttered. "I meant it, though. You've put on some muscle."

"That's what happens when you can't use your legs," Saber retorted.

Saber moved to one of the seats and strapped in. Sword and Thunder would be the pilots for the mission. While all of them were experienced, those two wouldn't send up red flags the way Saber, Hunter, and Dagger would. He leaned his head back, closed his eyes, and pulled Taylor's beautiful image into his mind.

Chapter 13

Six days later, Saber stood on Dises V. He turned as Razor approached. They had landed in a desolate area north of where the Trivator forces had set up their headquarters. Razor had been keeping them posted on what was happening.

"Razor," Saber said, nodding to him when he stopped in front of him.

"She and four other Trivator warriors have been tried and found guilty," Razor replied in response.

Saber hid the fact that he felt like Razor had just punched him. He could feel the nerve in his jaw pulsing. His hand wrapped around the knife at his waist.

"Where is she?" He asked in a deceptively quiet voice.

Saber didn't miss Razor's glance at the other men standing around them. Each warrior was poised and ready. The only thing they needed was a location.

"Let's take this inside," Razor replied, waving his hand to a temporary structure that had been set up. "A global field disrupter has been set up in orbit, but I don't want to take a chance."

Saber nodded and strode toward the large tent. The field disrupter was used to prevent their enemies from using the satellite or drone systems to lock on their location and movements. It was an excellent system, but required constant monitoring so that it wasn't hacked by their enemies and used against them.

He waited as Razor nodded to the table set up in the center room. Walking over, he sat down and stared at the holographic map of the planet floating in the center of the table. It was a rugged, mountainous planet.

"Earlier today, the Western sector sent a vidcom of a mock trial. They made sure that Taylor and the other four warriors were visible," Razor started to explain, tapping the console in front of him to display the video.

"The ruling sector of Dises V finds each of you guilty of treason," a voice off-screen said. *"Each warrior is sentenced to fight in the death rings."*

Saber's jaw tightened as the image flashed to each warrior's face. They all stared back at the front of the room in silence, their heads held high. For a brief moment, the video turned, showing five men standing up at the front of the room. Every man wore a cover over their face so that only their eyes showed. What they didn't know was that the eyes were the key to a man's soul. He would take the time later to study each one carefully.

He sat forward when the image turned to where Taylor was sitting off to the side. She was wearing a white shirt and a pair of dark tan pants. Her long hair was braided and the bruises on her face were healed. She looked incredibly young and fragile.

His gut twisted at the sight of her. He knew the men holding her were using her delicate appearance as a way to push their buttons. They wanted Razor to see that they could ruthlessly crush her if they wanted. She was a symbol of the Eastern sector… and the Trivators, powerless to stop their cruelty.

"State your name, traitor," the man demanded, stepping down from where he had been standing behind the table.

Taylor raised a delicate eyebrow and stared back at the man in defiance. A tug of amusement pulled at the corner of Saber's lips even as he wanted to strangle Taylor for being so stubborn. She might look delicate and fragile, but he knew she had the heart of a warrior.

"My name is not traitor, jackass. It is Taylor Sampson," she stated calmly, looking at the man. *"You know only cowards feel a need to hide their faces, don't you?"*

"You will only answer the questions," the man said in a harsh voice, taking a step closer to where she was sitting. *"You are under the protection of the Trivator known as Hunter, the brother of the one called Razor who has attacked our planet, are you not?"*

"Actually, Hunter is my brother-in-law," Taylor replied with a smile that didn't reach her eyes. *"Razor is going to kick your asses."*

Saber's hands curled into tight fists when the male stepped forward and slapped Taylor across the face. He heard Hunter and the others swiftly inhale their breath. That male was dead.

"Kill them if they move again," the man said, turning to look at where the four Trivator prisoners were straining to break free.

"It's okay, guys. Asswipe hits like a girl," Taylor said with a trembling smile. *"I've got this."*

"That female needs to be protected from herself," Sword muttered with a shake of his head. "Why would she say things that she knows will get her beaten?"

"Watch," Razor replied with a strangely calm demeanor.

Taylor turned back and stared at the man with a serene smile. A sense of unease built inside Saber. When Taylor looked like that, it usually meant trouble.

"I'm not the traitor to your people, you are," Taylor said in a quiet voice. *"You enslave them and work them until they die for your own greed. You and those that follow you are the scum of this planet. You are nothing more than parasites. If the people knew just how few of you there were, they'd squish you like the bugs you are."*

"I told you to answer only the questions you were asked!" The male said, raising his hand to strike her again.

Taylor took advantage of his closeness and kicked out, catching the man in the groin with a powerful kick. At the same time, she reached out and snatched off the cloth covering his face. The man twisted around, showing his full face clearly to the video. Two other men hurried forward and held Taylor by her arms.

"Answer that, you jerk-off!" She snapped before glancing up at the camera. *"Now that you know what he looks like, kill the bastard for me, please."*

The male on the ground hissed in pain as he struggled to sit up. He slowly rose, glaring at Taylor, who sat still, her head held high, waiting for his response. It didn't take long. He swung out, striking her in the jaw. Her head snapped back and she slumped in the chair, unconscious.

"Remove her," the man ordered. *"I look forward to killing her slowly, after I break her. Take them to the High Fortress. She is sentenced to death. I'll return her body to Razor one piece at a time. In the meantime, she can enjoy watching each of the Trivator warriors fight to their death."*

Saber sat back in his seat, stunned. Taylor, his Taylor, was still rebellious in the face of her captors. It reminded him of the way she had fought against him when she and her sisters had first been found. His hand rose to touch his ear, remembering her bite as if it was yesterday.

"I am surprised they sent that video," Hunter said in a quiet voice.

"They didn't… at first," Razor replied. "The first one we received was edited and did not contain this footage. This one arrived several hours later on a rarely used frequency. It would appear that either someone was sympathetic to Taylor or…"

"There is an ally among the new Western Council," Saber murmured, staring at the twisted face of the male that had hit Taylor.

He wasn't a Disesian. The milky white complexion and bald head were proof of that. Saber glanced at Dagger to see his reaction. Dagger's face had paled, but the fury burning deep inside him radiated outward. The Waxian, a mercenary species known for their greed and savagery, were trying to take over another planet.

"Where is the High Fortress?" Saber asked in a voice devoid of emotion.

Razor sighed and turned to look at the men. He shook his head and touched the console in front of him. A large mountain appeared in the center of the screen.

"This is the fortress we believe the Waxian was talking about," Razor said, pointing to the huge structure on the side of the mountain. "It is an ancient fortress built into the side of the mountain. We've been monitoring the increased traffic to it over the last several months."

"Why didn't you take it out?" Thunder asked, sitting back in his seat.

Razor's lips thinned in anger. "The council felt it would jeopardize the treaty that was under negotiation," he replied.

"Why the Waxians? How did they get a foothold into the Western Council?" Sword asked, leaning forward.

"The Western Council probably thought they would get additional support and weapons," Dagger said in a calm voice. He looked at each man at the table, pausing on Saber. "They would have taken over almost immediately, probably by taking the families of the council hostage and killing one or more of them as a warning. He meant what he said. He'll send pieces of Taylor to Razor just to show that he can. They are probably after the ore that is being mined. The unrest between the two regions, and the Alliance intervening, gave them an opportunity to steal it."

Razor nodded. "We believe the Waxians have struck a deal with a select group of Disesians to supply the Drethulans with the ore necessary to manufacture weapons. The Drethulans are not happy with the expansion of the Alliance into their territories. The Alliance Council believes that the Drethulans are building up their military," he explained.

"All-out war?" Dagger asked.

Razor glanced at all the men, pausing on Hunter who nodded. "None of this leaves this room," Razor said. "We've been working with a new species on the outer rim of the galaxy that recently joined the Alliance. They were the first to warn us of the Drethulans' military expansion. The Drethulans are not aware that we are working with the Kassisans. I suspect that the video we received came from one of their men. I suspect one of them has infiltrated the Drethulans' inner circle."

"I didn't think the Drethulans trusted anyone," Dagger retorted, leaning back in his seat.

Razor glanced at him before drawing in a deep breath. "They don't. I didn't ask how the Kassisan was able to gain their trust, I'm just glad he is on our side," he responded.

"Do you have a blueprint of the fortress?" Saber asked.

He had been silent while the rage that had started smoldering inside of him six days ago exploded, blazing inside him. Watching the Waxian strike Taylor had been the last straw. He would kill the bastard once he knew Taylor was safe.

"Saber, this is more than just Taylor," Razor started to say.

"No, it's not," Hunter interjected, watching warily as Saber rose from his seat. "This is Taylor, Razor. My *Amate's* sister."

"And mine," Dagger said, rising as well. "This is personal."

"Do you have a blueprint of the fortress?" Saber repeated in a cold voice.

Razor sighed and shook his head. "No, the Waxian was very careful about making sure all the recorders were destroyed. We have a basic diagram, and research from the time period the structure was built has given us additional probabilities on the layout."

"There will only be the six of us," Razor warned.

"Ten," Thunder said, pushing his chair back and standing. "Once we release the other four warriors."

"Plus the Kassisan," Sword added.

"Eleven, if we are lucky, against a hundred or more," Razor pointed out. "I've refused the Alliance Council's orders to send in the destroyers. There are too many civilians being held as hostages. Normally that wouldn't be an issue, but in this case, it is."

"Why?" Hunter asked with a raised eyebrow.

Razor grimaced. "Because this time it is personal," he admitted. "Jesse and Jordan both contacted me shortly before you arrived and made me swear to bring Taylor, and you two, home safe. I think Jordan hacked into your system again," he added dryly, glancing at Hunter.

"*Shewta*!" Hunter and Dagger muttered at the same time.

Chapter 14

Saber drew in a deep breath of the frigid air, embracing the chill of it in his lungs. It matched his icy resolve. He glanced over his shoulder when he saw Dagger walking toward him. Final preparations were being made for their departure. They would break up into teams and go in from different directions: Hunter and Razor, Thunder and Sword, he, Trig, and Dagger.

The plan was to find and rescue Taylor and the four warriors. Saber would take Taylor to safety while the other men systematically took out the Waxian forces.

Razor wanted to capture the bastard that struck Taylor. It was obvious he was the leader of the Waxians and Razor was determined to get all the information he knew about the Drethulans' current movements. Saber wanted to kill the male – slowly.

"The skids have arrived," Dagger said.

"I know," Saber replied, staring out across the barren landscape. "With the skids, Razor said it would take about an hour and a half to get there."

Dagger nodded. "It is the only way to ensure that we go in silent. Are you ready for this?" He asked.

Saber turned and glared at Dagger. "Are you asking if I'm capable of finding Taylor and getting her out?" He demanded in a harsh tone.

Dagger shook his head. "No," he replied in a quiet voice. "I know you can do that. I'm asking if you will keep it together once you find her. There is no telling what the Waxian has done to her. I know what they are capable of," he murmured, returning Saber's gaze with a steady one of his own. "He won't care that she is a female. If anything, he will be even crueler because he sees little value in her. She wouldn't last the first round in a fight ring."

Saber's jaw tightened. Dagger wasn't telling him anything he didn't already know. Taylor's move may have shown them the true faction behind the civil war that was raging between the two regions, but she had also sealed her fate. The Waxian would slowly drain the life out of her.

Both men turned when Hunter and Razor walked up to them. Saber noticed the grim expression on Razor's face. He waited, steeling himself for what Razor was about to tell them.

"I just received an update from our informant. He suggests that if we plan on saving the remaining prisoners, we strike now," Razor bit out in a harsh voice.

"Remaining?" Saber asked, his throat tightening.

Razor nodded. "The Waxian decided it was necessary to have a public showing of what happens to traitors," he explained in a voice laced with anger. "Several Eastern captives and one of the Trivator warriors named Ember fought two Gartaians. Ember was killed."

"Taylor?" Saber asked in a husky voice.

"She was forced to watch," Razor replied.

Saber drew in a hissing breath. "The Waxian is mine to kill," he said, looking at Razor.

Razor gave Saber a sharp-toothed grin. "After I get the information out of him, you can do what you want," he promised. "It is time to go. Our informant gave us some additional information about the fortress. There are three ancient drainage tunnels leading into it. I've uploaded the maps to your tablet. Taylor is being held in the uppermost turret. The remaining warriors and prisoners are being held in the underground cells."

"Saber and I will go after Taylor," Dagger said with a nod.

"Are you sure you can trust this Kassisan?" Saber asked, staring at Razor.

Razor shook his head. "No, but at this point, we don't have much choice," he replied, turning back toward the skids. "We'll split up five kilometers out."

..*

Taylor growled and kicked the door. A muted curse of pain escaped her. The only thing kicking a metal door did was hurt her foot. Hopping, she briefly rubbed it with her left hand before releasing it to stand and gaze around the room.

"I'm going to roast that guy's balls in the hottest oven I can find," she muttered as she stared at the bare room.

There wasn't even a bed in the room, or a blanket! Hell, they hadn't even given her a pot to pee in. Her nose wiggled in distaste. Her gaze rose to the narrow window. The fortress was just that, an ancient fortress that was built back in the stone age of the planet. It looked like some of those buildings she had studied when she was back on Earth.

She stepped back, gazing up at the narrow slit. Turning, she looked at the other three that were designed to allow fresh air and a small measure of light into the room. She raised her hand, trying to gage how wide they were.

Biting her lip, she debated if she should try to escape. She turned back to the door and sighed. There was no way she was getting out that way. The door was made of the thick metal that the Disesians had mined. The stuff was incredibly strong.

And hurt like hell when you kicked it, she thought in disgust.

"Well, I'm not just going to sit around and let that crazy bastard use me as monster food," she muttered with a shudder.

This morning's time in the 'arena' had shown her exactly how she didn't want to die. Her eyes burned as she remembered the poor souls that had died as the small audience cheered. She brushed a hand across her chin to wipe away the tear that escaped and winced in pain. She forgot about the lovely bruise she had. She had lied to the camera. The ass-wipe didn't hit like a girl.

"I can do this," she whispered, eyeing the northern window.

She backed up and played out how many moves she would have to make to reach it. Fortunately, the inside of the room was not as finished as the rest of the fortress.

"Thank goodness they got tired of polishing walls by the time they built this stupid part," she muttered, shaking out her legs and arms. "Just remember what Kali said; use the formation of the building to help you get up to where you want to go."

Drawing in a deep breath, she sprinted forward. Jumping, she used the uneven walls to give her hands and feet something to hold onto. She pushed off, using her leg muscles to give her the added boost. Her fingers scraped the ledge of the window before she felt gravity working against her, pulling her back down to the floor.

She twisted and landed with her knees bent, rolling on her left shoulder and coming back up onto her feet in a crouching position. Shaking out the trembling in her limbs, she rose to her feet and focused again. This was just like when she was in gymnastics and learning a new routine.

She cleared her mind of everything but the move until she could see was each step of it. Breathing deeply, she rocked back and forth until she could feel the timing was right. Sprinting, she jumped again. She ignored the pain in her fingers as the rough rock cut into them.

Her fingers gripped the edge. She gritted her teeth as she held herself for a brief second before she pushed up with her toes. She was panting by the time she finally got up far enough to look out the narrow opening. She kicked her feet until she could wiggle enough to sit on the sill.

She looked out over the landscape. The moon lit the area with just enough light to give her a pretty good view of the terrain below. The lower areas were dark. She'd discovered there wasn't any electricity installed in the fortress when she was being moved from one part of the building to another. All lighting had to be done using either generators or the good old-fashioned torch method. All she knew was that it would work in her favor when escaping.

She glanced down at her hands with a grimace before leaning far enough out the window to see what was below her. Her eyes widened when she saw a flat roof with a hatch a little over ten feet down from the tower window. There were also long pieces of timber sticking out from where the tower was built.

"Awesome!" She whispered, glancing at the door and giving it a one finger salute. "Hasta la vista, jerk wads."

Scooting up until she was standing, she carefully turned in the opening and lowered herself down until she was on her stomach with her legs hanging over the side. Holding on to the lip, she felt around with her right foot until she felt wood.

She slid her foot back and forth until she felt confident she could put both feet down without losing her balance. Shifting her weight, she slowly lowered her body onto the narrow beam sticking out of the wall. Holding onto the wall as best she could, she glanced over her shoulder and swallowed.

"Just think of it as a balance beam," she whispered. "You can do this, Taylor. You kicked ass at the National Championship."

She glanced down over her right shoulder. Six feet. She could do this. The roof was only about six feet down. Turning carefully, she drew in a deep breath and focused. Counting to three, she lowered herself down onto the two foot section of wood, balancing herself as she squatted down, placing her hands between her legs until she could sit on the wood.

Blowing out her breath, she placed her left hand on the outside of her thigh and twisted, centering her weight, and awkwardly lowered herself down. She worked her body around until she was lying across the wood. Scooting backwards again, she felt for the next piece of wood with the toe of her boot.

"One more, then you can jump," she told herself, trying to boost her confidence.

She lowered her weight onto it, and gasped when the edge of the wood gave way. She bit the inside of her cheek to keep from crying out and alerting someone. Her hands instinctively reached up to grab the section she had just been on while her feet frantically scrambled to find a section of the wood that wasn't rotten.

It took several times before she finally found a small foothold. It wouldn't be enough to hold her. Glancing over her shoulder, she let go, twisting as she fell. Her arms swung out to try to keep her upright. She bent her legs and rolled when she hit the wooden planksroof of the small lookout. Within seconds of landing, she knew why no one was there when the roof made a cracking noise before it disintegrated underneath her weight.

Taylor covered her head with her arms as she fell through the opening. She landed on her back amid the dust created by the rotted wood made from centuries of neglect. She moaned and rolled, trying to cover her nose and mouth at the same time as she drew in gasping breaths to replenish the air knocked out of her. Smothering a cough, she finally rolled onto her back again and gaze up at the dark sky.

She waited to see if the noise had attracted any attention. The only sounds she heard came from the occasional piece of wood that still fell and the wind. Breathing a sigh of relief, she winced as she sat up. Rubbing her left hip, she rose shakily to her feet and stared up at the tower window that she had just escaped from.

It sure does look a lot higher from down here than it did from up there, she thought as she stiffly straightened.

Glancing down, she carefully picked her way over the collapsed roof to the stairs. A look of doubt crossed her face as she stared down at them. They didn't look like they were in much better shape than the roof.

"Oh well," she whispered, straightening her shoulders. "It isn't like you have a lot of choice in the matter."

Bracing her hand against the wall, she slowly began her descent, testing each step before she actually put all her weight on it. *At the rate I am going, I should reach the bottom by my ninetieth birthday,* she thought with disgust as the darkness closed in around her.

..*

Saber leaned forward on the skid, pushing it to the limit. The vehicle silently sped across the desert floor, reaching speeds of close to six hundred kilometers per hour. The actual travel time to reach the bottom of the mountain would only be an hour and a half. The additional time would be scaling the sides undetected and breaching the interior walls through the three separate drainage tunnels.

An hour and twenty minutes later, Thunder and Sword turned to the northeast as the mountain came into view. Ten minutes later, Hunter and Razor turned in the opposite direction. Saber, Dagger, and Trig remained fixed on their heading, slowing to a crawl five minutes afterward as the rocky base of the mountain prevented them from traveling any faster.

"The entrance to the drainage tunnel should be just ahead," Dagger informed him.

"I see it," Saber replied, pulling back on the throttle and bringing the skid to a stop. "Nine meters up and to your left."

Saber climbed off the skid and walked over to a series of rocks that had fallen over the years. Reaching up, he gripped a protruding section and began climbing. Under his uniform he could feel the brace activate. The pulsation caused the muscles to contract and release, stabilizing his leg.

"You good?" Trig asked, joining him.

Saber shot Trig a heated glance. "Does it look like I'm having trouble?" He snapped in annoyance.

Trig grinned and shook his head. "No. I might need to look into that brace," he said, pulling himself up. "I swear I'm getting too old for this shit. Why can't the bad guys hide out in easier locations?"

"Because they wouldn't make very good bad guys," Dagger retorted, climbing ahead of his brother.

All three men moved like silent ghosts up the rock face to the entrance. An old iron-ore gate covered the opening. Saber pulled a laser cutter out of the equipment pouch at his waist and sliced through it. Dagger and Trig grabbed the piece, holding it steady for a moment before they lowered it to the ground.

"That's a heavy piece of shit," Dagger muttered as he let go and stood up.

Saber nodded. "That is why the Drethulans want it. The weapons are heavy, but they'll survive just about anything," he replied under his breath.

"Great! Just what we need, those weird worm-shifters with armor," Trig grumbled with a shudder. "Be thankful you missed that fight, Dagger."

Dagger shook his head. "I fought just about everything else," he reminded Trig before moving to the side so Saber could go ahead of them.

"Sometimes you need to learn when to shut up," Saber informed Trig under his breath before he stepped around him.

Saber adjusted the MMOS, or Multi-mode-optical Scanner, goggles he had worn during the trip to help him see in the increased darkness. Touching the side, he scanned for any alarms. The scan came up negative.

"They must not have done their homework as well as the Kassisan did," Dagger murmured, stepping in behind him and letting Trig take the rear.

"It makes me wonder what else the Kassisan knows and hasn't told us," Saber retorted as he stepped over some debris that had washed down from the drainage above.

Chapter 15

Taylor remained frozen against the wall. She hoped the guard didn't turn and come down the small hallway where she had hidden the moment she heard him coming. She shivered, also hoping there were no creepy crawlies hiding in the narrow passage with her.

She was exhausted, but fear was giving her the strength to continue. It had taken her a good hour or more to get out of the lower tower. So far, none of her captors appeared to be aware that she had escaped. One look at the roof of the shorter tower and they probably assumed that she had fallen to her death!

More power to them if they try to go find my body, she thought nastily. *If I had weighed an ounce more, the whole damn stairwell would have come down on me.*

She had difficulties coming down the rickety stairs and had slightly sore ankles to prove it! Her feet had gone through at least three rotten steps. The others had just been missing. That wouldn't have been a problem if she could have seen where in the heck she was putting her feet.

Sighing as the guard disappeared down the hallway, Taylor rose and slid along the wall to peek around the corner. She silently retraced her steps from this morning. After what happened to those poor men and women at the arena in the dome, she knew she couldn't leave the other prisoners behind.

She paused and carefully removed an old torch from the wall. It had a foot-long piece of metal at the bottom. She felt along the wood and was relieved when she felt that it was nice and strong.

Turning it so that the metal end was facing away from her, she held it like a bat. Once again, she sent a word of thanks to the great unknown for giving her a chance to participate in a wide variety of sports. She leaned forward to peek around the corner once more before slipping out from her hiding spot.

Prymorus Achler, the Waxian, had been totally full of himself when he ordered the guards to escort her and the others to a small arena that they had built in the lower courtyard. It had been a huge, metal domed area. Six people, one Trivator warrior that she'd learned was called Ember, two women, and three other men had been pushed into the cage.

Nausea rose in Taylor's throat as she remembered the slaughter. Two of the men had grabbed one of the women and held her between them. Ember and the other man had tried to help the woman while the other cried pitifully against the bars, holding out her arms and pleading for mercy.

That was when the gate had opened and two mammoth creatures her Waxians captors had called Gartaians, had been released into the cage. Taylor and the others watched in hopeless horror as the creatures ripped the woman held between the two men apart as they fought over her.

It had been a hopeless battle. None of the captives had been given a weapon. They had no way of defending themselves against the two creatures that stood almost four meters high and weighed in at over ten thousand kilograms.

The first two men attacked the other woman, ripping her away from the bars as she screamed and fought in an effort to shove her in front of them and keep the creature from attacking them. One of the beasts swung his massive head, piercing the screaming woman with one of the three tusks protruding from its mouth. The other Gartaian's tongue swept out and dragged the impaled woman off the tusk and into its mouth. The sickening sound of bone being crushed had been too much for Taylor. She couldn't watch any more.

Instead, she'd focused on how she was going to escape. She wouldn't die in that cage, being eaten by some alien monster. She would rather take her chances of being killed while trying to escape, than end up being torn apart. Still, she couldn't escape without trying to free the others. As far as she was concerned, the only one who deserved to die that way was Achler. She'd love to see how he liked being put in a cage with a Gartaian or two.

Rubbing her damp cheek on her shoulder, she winced when she swiped the bruise again. An angry scowl replaced her grief. She'd also like to hit the bastard upside the jaw with the end of a baseball bat. If she ever got a chance to kick him in the balls again, she was going to make sure they ended up in his throat! She hoped that the marble size jewels choked him, but not before the Gartaian ripped him apart.

She paused at the end of the corridor. Her eyes narrowed on the guard. He was taking a leak in the corner. The strong smell of urine filled the hallway. Gripping the torch, she silently stepped up behind him. She swung the end of the torch just as he was closing the front of his pants.

Taylor watched as the man spun around as if in slow motion before collapsing to the cold stone floor. Squatting down, she quickly searched him for the keys. She wiggled her nose at the offensive smell coming off the man, but continued to pat him down until she felt a bulky, metal object just under his left side. She set the torch down next to her and shifted him just far enough to pull the ring of keys out from under him. Grabbing the torch, she glanced at the man once more before rolling her eyes.

Weapons! He's bound to have at least one on him, she thought in disgust.

Setting the torch and keys down, she stood up and rolled him over. Holding her breath, she absently wondered when was the last time the man had taken a bath. Deciding it must have been a long time, she pulled the weapon tucked in the front of his pants out with two fingers and grimaced.

"This is just nasty," she muttered, bending and picking up the keys and torch again.

She sighed when she realized that she couldn't hold all three items if she wanted to stay quiet. A shudder went through her as she tucked the laser pistol into the back of her pants. She was just thankful she was wearing a long shirt and panties. The thought of it touching her skin was too repulsive for words. She tucked the keys into the front of her pants and gripped the torch firmly between her palms again.

Feeling more confident, she continued down the corridor. One more hallway and she would be in the lower catacombs where the other prisoners were being held. She just hoped there weren't any more guards.

Swallowing, she couldn't help but think of Saber. How he did something like this for years on end, she didn't know. Sure, she and her sisters had been on the run, but they spent more of their time hiding. This warrior stuff was just too nerve-wracking for her. She pressed her lips together into a tight line to keep from making any noise. When all this was over, Saber had better be ready to hold her good and tight for a long, long time, because she didn't plan on ever leaving his arms again.

..*

Saber stood in the center of the tower, looking around. Dagger grunted as he dragged the body of the dead guard into the room. Saber turned, looking at the male they had killed.

"She was supposed to be here," he growled out in anger, glaring at the male as if he could wring more information from him.

"The guard was positioned outside the door to the room and another one at the bottom of the tower," Dagger replied, glancing around the barren area. "Why post guards here if she wasn't?"

Saber shook his head, searching the chamber once more. His eyes narrowed on the boot imprints on the floor. Walking around in a tight circle, he studied the pattern. He squatted down and ran his fingers along the thin layer of dirt. The footprints belonged to Taylor. They were too small to belong to anyone else. There were a couple of places where the imprints were smeared, as if she had dragged the ball of her foot across the floor.

His eyes swept the uneven surface. The footprints were stretched apart. It looked like she was running. His gaze continued following the pattern. Rising, he walked toward the wall, his mind trying to understand what his eyes were seeing. He stopped at the wall. About half way up it, he could see the outline of the toe of her boot.

Saber frowned as his gaze rose upward, freezing on the window. A silent curse tore from his throat as the puzzle pieces that Taylor had left behind started to fit together. Turning, he motioned for Dagger to join him.

"What is it?" Dagger asked with a frown.

"Cup your hands and give me a boost," Saber demanded, stepping back so Dagger could move up under the window.

"What for?" Dagger asked, cupping his hands and bracing his feet. "Damn, Trig is right, you've gained weight."

"Taylor's not in here because she escaped," Saber whispered, reaching up and grabbing the window sill.

Holding his body still, he scanned the area. A hoarse curse escaped him when he saw the building down below them. He was about to tell Dagger to lower him back down when the faint scent of blood caught his attention. Leaning down, he sniffed the edge of the window. Explosive anger burst through him. With a grunt, he motioned for Dagger to lower him back to the floor.

"Well?" Dagger asked.

"She went out the window," Saber said, turning on his heel and striding out the door.

"Out the...," Dagger started to say before he turned and hurried after Saber.

Saber took the curving stairs at a reckless speed. Trig turned, looking startled, when he flashed by him. A frown creased Trig's brow when Dagger came down a moment later.

"What happened?" Trig asked, following them.

Dagger glanced at his brother and shook his head. "She escaped," he muttered with a slightly exasperated tone. "Goddess only knows where she is now!"

Chapter 16

Taylor shuddered as another guard collapsed. Her hope that there wouldn't be any more guards dissolved when she unexpectedly collided with one as they were both rounding a corner in the lower catacomb.

She had reacted instinctively, raising her knee and driving it into his groin. The guard's surprise at her sudden appearance and her immediate reaction were the only things that gave her the edge. A harsh curse escaped him at about the same time as the wave of pain washed through his body at her blow. His eyes had widened in shock before he bent forward and grabbed his groin. As he sank down to the floor, she had stepped back and swung the end of the torch. The blow had caught him in the temple and he toppled over.

"PT Taylor," one of the Trivator warriors called out.

Taylor jerked in surprise to hear her name and grinned. Stepping over the unconscious guard, she fumbled for the keys she had retrieved from the other man. Within seconds, she had the locks to the cells open.

"We've got to get out of here," she said, glancing at the guard she had just knocked out. "There was another one upstairs. I'm not sure how long he is going to be out."

The sound of shouts from above sent a shaft of fear through her. The guard had either been found or had raised an alert. She watched as the Trivator warrior named Cain hurried over to the unconscious man and searched him. He pulled a weapon from the man's waist.

Taylor looked away when he stepped back and fired a shot into the man's temple. There would be no prisoners from the look on the men's faces. Pulling the other laser pistol from the back of her pants, she held it out to the other Trivator warrior that she remembered was called Ace.

"We need to find a way out of here," one of the Eastern captives said in desperation.

"Follow me," a voice said, stepping out of the darkness behind Taylor.

Taylor gasped when she felt the cold metal of a pistol against her temple. She wanted to turn her head, but at the moment, she didn't dare. She was trapped between the man holding the gun to her head and the two warriors pointing their pistols in the direction of her chest.

"Shoot!" She whispered before stiffening. "I didn't mean it that way. Don't shoot. I meant this is not where I want to be, not that I want you to really shoot! Argh! Just shut up already, Taylor!"

A soft chuckle in her ear sent another shiver down her spine. She was glad someone was finding this amusing. Her eyes widened when the two warriors raised their weapons.

"I know a way out of here," the man said. "There are also more Trivators in the fortress. I would suggest if you want to get out of here that you listen."

"You lie!" Ace snarled.

"No, he doesn't," another voice said.

Taylor looked out of the corner of her eye. Two more warriors that she didn't recognize stepped out from the darkness. She staggered back against the wall when the pistol at her temple disappeared and the man stepped to the side. Swallowing, she turned and backed up until she was standing behind the two Trivator warriors she did know.

"Thunder! Sword!" Cain and Ace both hissed at the same time. "How many forces are here?"

"Seven warriors, plus you two," Thunder replied, glancing at the group. His eyebrow rose when he saw Taylor peeking out from behind the men. "We were told that you were locked in the tower."

The man who'd held the gun on her shrugged his shoulders. She couldn't see his face because he had it covered with the same headdress that Achler wore. A shiver went through her when he nodded his head at her.

"She was supposed to be," he said. "She escaped."

"How did you…?" She started to say when she heard the sound of footsteps running in their direction.

"Time to go," the man said, waving his hand toward the end of a short corridor. "There is another hallway at the end. Turn left. It will take you to the underground drainage system. Go!"

"What about the other warriors?" Cain asked, ignoring the fact that the other prisoners were already running down the corridor."

"I will assist them as much as I can without compromising my assignment," the man replied through gritted teeth.

"Which other warriors?" Taylor asked with a sinking feeling in her stomach just as several of Achler's men came around the corner.

"Go!" Cain yelled, turning and firing at the guards.

The man who had held the gun to her head pulled on her arm. He raised his own weapon, firing two shots and killing the other two guards. Taylor looked on in confusion as she was forced to turn down the short corridor.

"What about those men?" She asked as she jogged down the passage.

The man shrugged his shoulder and pushed her when she started to turn around. The group of captives was frantically trying to figure out where to go at the end of the second corridor. Taylor heard the man release a savage curse.

"The floor! You are standing on the drainage gate," he pointed out. "You! I'm putting you in charge. Open the gate and help the women down. Keep to the left at all sections. You will eventually come to the base of the mountains. You are on your own from there. If you head east, there is a rebel camp not far over the border in the Mountains of the Crescent Moon."

The man nodded and hurriedly waved the others off the grate. He and three of the men pulled it back, letting it drop with a clatter to the side. One of the men sat down on the edge before jumping, another quickly followed. Within seconds, the women were disappearing through the grate.

"Wait! Where are you going?" Taylor asked when the strange man started to turn back the way they came.

"I have to get back upstairs without being seen," he replied with a frustrated sigh, turning to pierce her with his dark purple eyes. "I've compromised my position as it is. I should have killed all of you instead of taking the chance to free you. Now, I need to go save the lives of a couple of crazy Trivator councilmen."

"Councilmen!" Taylor exclaimed, her eyes widening.

"Yes, now in case you haven't noticed, there is a battle going on," the man replied sarcastically.

Taylor nodded and stood back. Her gaze flickered to the man guiding the captives. There were five left, not counting her. In the background, she could hear the sound of the Gartaians snorting and…

"Come on," the man said, standing alone.

Taylor started, but something held her back. She heard something. She glanced at the man. He was staring back at her with an impatient frown. She started to take a step when she heard the sound again. It sounded like the soft cry of a child.

"I hear something," Taylor said, looking with a plea at the man. "Don't you hear it?"

"No. Listen, if you are coming with us, you need to do it now," the man said.

Taylor took a step back and shook her head when he started to reach out for her. Now that she knew what she was listening to, it was clear that not everyone had been freed. Shaking her head, she backed away from the drainage hole.

"You go," she said. "I'll catch up. There is someone else still here."

The man glanced down at the hole, then at her, before he shrugged his shoulders. "I have to think of the others," he said in apology before he sat on the edge and disappeared through the opening.

Taylor headed back down the short corridor and turned right. The fighting sounded like it was moving upward. She paused at the end of the long passage to make sure it was clear. Her gaze swept over dead guards. Turning away, she listened. The crying sounded like it had come from further down the arched corridor.

She gripped the torch she was still holding tightly in her hand and followed the sound. At the end, she could see the entrance to the dome where Achler had released the Gartaians earlier this morning. Her footsteps slowed as she drew closer. She could hear the creatures in their cages nearby snorting and moving restlessly, but there had been another sound, she was sure of it.

She almost missed the door where the crying was coming from. A small square window with bars across stood eye level. She paused and looked down the hallway again before she walked forward and peered into the dark room.

"Who's there?" She whispered, holding the torch up in case she needed it.

"PT Taylor?" A small voice sniffed.

Taylor's eyes widened in horror as a familiar face came into view. The shaggy sand-colored hair, dark brown eyes, and pale, dirty face stared back at her in silence. Her heart melted at the look of hope in his eyes.

"Oh, Lonnie!" She whispered, reaching for the metal bar locking him in.

Chapter 17

Saber moved in silence, striking down any unlucky guard that stood in his way. Fear, anger, and a touch of exasperation with Taylor, fought for dominance inside him. Why he was surprised that she would not only try to escape, but succeed at it, was beyond him.

They had worked their way over to the lower tower to make sure she hadn't broken her fool neck. Saber had picked up the slight scent of her the moment they entered the lower entryway. The tracks of her boots in the accumulated dirt proved that she had made it down the stairway.

"She's lucky she didn't kill herself," Dagger had muttered as the three of them stood at the bottom of the dilapidated wooden staircase.

"That's a long way up there," Trig added, rubbing the back of his neck. "She's as crazy as Jordan."

Dagger punched his brother in the arm. "Jordan's not crazy," he growled.

Trig rubbed his arm and scowled at Dagger. "What have you been doing? Working out with Saber?" He complained with a raised eyebrow. "I swear I've been off-world too much."

"Let's go," Saber said, turning back to the entrance.

He paused at the doorway, glancing over the courtyard. He heard Dagger's muttered curse when it suddenly lit up with spotlights. Something told him that they weren't the only ones searching for Taylor now. He reached over his shoulder and pulled the laser rifle free from his back holster.

"They are converging on the lower level where Thunder and Sword were heading," Trig said, gripping a rifle in his hands.

"What the… *Shewta*!" All three men cursed when the guards that had been running toward the lower level of the fortress suddenly turned and retreated.

Saber understood why a moment later when a Gartaian squeezed through the narrow opening, tearing mortar as it pushed its way out. He paled when he saw the small figure running behind the beast.

"Taylor!" He hissed.

"*Shewta*! Trig's right, she *is* crazier than Jordan," Dagger muttered.

Saber didn't wait to hear Trig's response. He charged out into the courtyard, firing at the guards that were shooting at the Gartaian. His heart pounded when he saw Taylor pause to help a small boy who had stumbled while running alongside her.

Saber darted to the left and rolled when the Gartaian's long tusks struck out. He continued to roll until he was back on his feet. Behind him, a guard's scream was cut short as he was lifted by the long trunk of the beast. The guard in front of him twisted as a blast caught him in the chest. Saber glanced over his shoulder just in time to see Dagger aiming for another guard.

His left arm swung out and he caught Taylor around the waist as she started to turn back around. Her frightened scream trailed off and a look of astonishment crossed her face when she recognized who had grabbed her. He bent and scooped up the small boy she had by the hand with his other arm, continuing his sprint across the open courtyard until he reached the curved stone archways near where Taylor had emerged.

He released the boy, pressing him back against the stone, and raised his rifle. He fired several rapid shots at the three guards who were running toward him. Twisting, he caught a fourth man across the yard. He turned again, this time barely stopping before he shot Dagger and Trig.

"Get her out of here," Trig ordered, firing at several more men. "Razor and Hunter are working on the top section. They are trying to find the Waxians."

"Achler," Taylor said, pushing herself up on Saber's back. "He's the leader. I left his ass down in the catacombs. I had to release one of the Gartaians on him so he couldn't get me and Lonnie."

"You had to…," Saber started to snarl.

He set Taylor down on her feet and pressed her up against the stone archway. A laser blast cut through the edge of the mortar, forcing all of them to seek cover. Trig and Dagger each took a side and returned fire. From above, Saber could see Razor running along the top walkway, firing on those below.

"Thunder and Sword are heading this way," Trig said, firing again.

Both men swerved behind one of the arches as several loud explosions shook the fortress. "Several transports have taken off," Sword said, breathing deeply. "A large group of Waxians escaped."

"They haven't left yet," Saber said as he raised his rifle and fired on one of the attack transports. "Incoming!" He yelled.

Saber pulled Taylor and the boy away from the wall and covered them with his body as the ship fired on the Gartaian. The creature screamed before collapsing. Turning sideways, he glanced over his shoulder.

Another ship fired on the tall tower where Taylor had been held. Within seconds, the second ship began firing on the fortress. They were systematically destroying it and anyone left inside. Saber's head jerked around when he saw Hunter, Razor, and the two Trivator warriors running across the courtyard.

"Fire!" He ordered as he turned the rest of the way and began providing coverage for them.

All five men opened up on the two transports. One of the warriors stumbled when a guard shot him. Saber turned and took the man out before refocusing on the fighter.

"Get inside!" Saber yelled as the men rushed under the archway.

He moved backwards, firing before turning and grabbing Lonnie up in his arms. He shielded Taylor as she followed Hunter, Razor, and the other men back inside the fortress. Dagger and Trig followed next with Sword and Thunder taking up the rear.

"Keep going," Saber shouted over the sound of explosions. "They are leveling the place."

Saber felt his body being pushed forward into Taylor as a rocket hit the entrance. The force of the blast threw them all to the floor. His arm wrapped protectively around Taylor's small waist and he tried to cushion the impact as best he could with the boy in his other arm.

It took several minutes before his ears quit ringing and the dust settled enough that he could talk. Under him, he could feel Taylor drawing in deep breaths and feel the trembling of the boy. Both told him that they were at least alive.

"Are you hurt?" Saber asked in a husky voice, his lips pressed against her left ear.

Taylor shook her head. He carefully released the boy and shifted far enough to turn Taylor over so that he could see her face. He wanted, needed, to make sure that she was alright for himself.

His hand rose and he carefully brushed her hair back from her face, waiting for her to open her eyes. Relief flooded him when he saw her eyelashes flutter before lifting. His fingers moved down to caress her bruised jaw before he bent his head and pressed his lips hungrily to hers.

He reluctantly pulled back when he felt a pair of eyes looking at him. Turning his head slightly, he locked gazes with a pair of curious brown eyes. He raised his eyebrow in inquiry.

"What?" He asked, staring back at the boy.

"I hope you aren't going to do that to me," he said with a look of disgust.

Hoarse laughter echoed in the dark chamber. Sighing, he rolled to the side and rose to his feet. He rubbed his hand down his right leg, thankful for the brace when he bent down to help Taylor to her feet. He could see the question in her eyes in the dim glow of the torch Razor had activated.

"How did you find me?" She whispered, reaching up to touch his cheek.

Saber was about to answer when another shock wave from a blast caused sections of rock to fall. He glanced up at the roof of the cavern they were in. Deep fissures were opening up under the onslaught. Reaching down, he grabbed his rifle.

"We need to get out of here," he said, looking around.

"There is a drainage grate in the lower catacomb that we can use," Cain said, nodding to Razor and Hunter in respect. "One of the Waxians pointed it out to us, though I don't know why. He said that you both were here, and Thunder and Sword confirmed that he was telling the truth."

"When?" Hunter asked in surprise.

"Can they share what happened later? I'd like to get out of here before the ceiling collapses on us," Trig suggested, waving his hand to Cain. "We'll follow you."

Cain nodded and turned. Saber watched as the two Trivators that had been held prisoner led the way through the long center corridor before turning to the right where a stone staircase was cut into the rock. He wrapped his arm protectively around Taylor when more of the ceiling collapsed behind them.

"I'm scared, PT Taylor," Lonnie whispered when the darkness of the winding staircase engulfed them.

"We're here for you, Lonnie," Taylor replied, reaching out and laying her hand on his thin shoulder. "How did you get here? I thought Buzz took you to the transport to be evacuated."

"PT Buzz did, but I didn't want to leave my mom," Lonnie replied with a sniff. "I couldn't find her."

"She is safe," Taylor assured him. "She was looking for you, but her dress got caught and she couldn't get it undone. I helped her and Buzz made sure she made it to one of the transports. She thought you were on one that had already left. I know she must be worried about you."

Lonnie sniffed again. "I miss her," he admitted in a quivering voice.

"We will return you to her," Saber promised, his voice sounding unusually loud in the narrow passage.

"Hold," Ace said, holding up his hand. "Do you hear that?" He murmured.

"It's the other Gartaian," Taylor said, pulling Lonnie back against her.

Cain nodded. "It looks like the wider passage leading up has been blasted. It was probably done in an attempt to keep them from escaping," he said, pointing the light in the direction of the wide arched corridor. The pillars had been destroyed about half way up and the roof collapsed.

"We can try shooting it, but with just the rifles, it won't do much damage," Ace said, glancing around.

"Where is the drainage grate?" Saber asked with a frown.

"On the other side of the Gartaian," Cain muttered.

"What if we set a laser rifle to overload?" Razor asked, studying the beast.

Trig shook his head. "Two things: one, it would have to be attached to the thing, and two, it would more than likely bring down the entire area," he said with a crooked grin. "I tried something similar on Teris VI."

"What if we locked it in the dome?" Taylor asked, looking around at the men.

Hunter shook his head. "How? It isn't likely to want to go in on its own," he responded, studying the beast.

"If there was a way to leave a scent trail of blood, it might work," Saber suggested.

Dagger raised his eyebrow at Saber. "I don't see any lying around and I sure as hell don't want that thing getting a scent of my blood," he said with a shudder. "I've already been in a cage with those things. I have no desire to do it ever again."

"Look out," Hunter yelled, reaching for Lonnie and picking him up as a large section of the upper staircase gave way and came tumbling down through the opening.

Saber grabbed Taylor, lifting her up and flattening his body against the side of the wall along the ledge that ran along the floor. The other men had scattered in an attempt to avoid the crushing avalanche of rocks.

"Whatever we are going to do, we've got to do it soon. Those fighter transports are making sure that none of us survive," Razor bit out as he turned his gaze up at the ceiling before looking back at where the Gartaian was moving its head restlessly back and forth.

"Let me down," Taylor whispered against Saber's ear.

Saber nodded. He reluctantly slid her body down his, but kept his hands on her hips. Bending his head, he brushed his lips across the top of her head.

"We need to talk when we get out of here," he murmured.

Taylor tilted her head back and smiled up at him. "Yes, we do," she said, running her hand down over his hip. "But first, we need to get out of here."

Saber frowned when she pulled away from him and stepped down on a fallen block of stone. She turned and smiled at him again. His frown deepened when he saw her raise her arm. His fingers went instinctively to his side where he kept his knife. It was gone.

"Taylor!" Saber growled as it dawned on him what she was about to do.

"I can do this," she whispered as she slid the sharp blade along her arm before dropping the knife and taking off at a run.

"TAYLOR!" Saber roared, jumping down off the ledge and grabbing his knife.

He watched in disbelief as Taylor ran toward the Gartaian, waving her bloody arm and yelling. The other men cursed and started forward, their rifles raised, but afraid to shoot in case they struck Taylor. The Gartaian raised its head and sniffed the air. The fresh smell of blood drove the beast into a frenzy. Its trunk swung around as it tried to pinpoint where the scent was coming from.

"I told you she was crazy," Trig muttered as he tried to get a shot in the narrow corridor.

Chapter 18

Taylor didn't know why she did what she did, it just suddenly dawned on her what needed to be done if they were going to get out of there. Out of all of them, she was the most likely to be successful at the stupid, crazy stunt she was about to do. There were two things that she knew for certain: one, she didn't want to get eaten, and, two, she was pretty sure from the sharp bite in Saber's voice, she was not likely to hear the end of it if she survived.

She hadn't cut very deep along her arm, but it stung. Her hand groped for her sleeve and she tugged on it, trying to rip it free as she ran. Finding a thin line cut through it, she pulled. It took three tries before she heard the sound of tearing.

"Hey, here you go," she yelled, waving her arm so that it could catch the scent of her blood. "Dumbo! Yeah, you! Come and get it!"

Taylor ignored the curses of the men. They were yelling for her to run. She wanted to yell back that she was, but didn't want to lose her focus.

She rolled when the long trunk of the creature swung out. Rising to her hands and feet, she crawled under its belly as it searched wildly for her. She jumped to her feet once she was on the other side.

Ripping the rest of her sleeve off, she waved it like a flag and continued yelling. The Gartaian might be almost blind, but it had an excellent sense of smell. She almost fell when it suddenly swung around.

"That's it," she said, waving the sleeve slowly back and forth as she backed away from the huge beast. "Come on, lard butt, you know you want it."

Taylor continued stepping down the corridor until the creature roared and charged. Turning on her heel, she bolted toward the end of the hall and the open door to the dome. She swept through the door and continued across the floor of the arena. Dropping her bloody sleeve in the center of it, she jumped the last few feet, grabbing the thick bars, and climbed upward as fast as she could. Near the top, she twisted and used her hands to cross the curved dome like it was a set of monkey bars.

She glanced down as she passed over the top of the creature. It had its head down and was trying to wrap its trunk around the remains of her sleeve. She was almost past it when its head suddenly jerked up. A loud curse escaped Saber. He was standing just inside the entrance to the dome with the laser rifle pressed against his shoulder.

"Don't shoot!" She cried out, pulling her legs up when the beast's trunk swung upward just under them. "All it will do is make the Gartaian mad and it might escape."

"Get her out of there!" Dagger yelled as he and Thunder ran around the other side of the dome.

Taylor raised her legs again, locking her feet through the bars and flattening her body as close as she could against the top when the Gartaian rose up on its back legs. She turned her head and bit her lip to keep from screaming when she felt it run the cold tip of its trunk along her back.

"Come here, you ugly bastard!" Dagger shouted, waving his arm inside the cage.

Taylor turned and looked upside down at Dagger. He had run a long cut along his arm, deeper than the one she had drawn with the knife and was waving his blood-covered limb as bait. She watched in horror as the creature lowered itself and charged.

Dagger pulled back just before it struck the bars. The impact shook the dome with such a force that it knocked Dagger backwards over the bench seating and knocked Taylor's feet free from where she had them braced. A scream tore from her throat as she started to fall. Her right hand wrapped around the bar and she swung in a crazy arc for a moment before she was able to grab the bar again with her left hand.

"Taylor, move it!" Saber roared as the Gartaian rose drunkenly to its feet.

Taylor swallowed down her fear and swiftly continued down the other side of the dome. She was almost fifteen feet up when the creature roared again. Glancing over her shoulder, she could see it twist around, this time facing her.

"Let go!" Saber ordered.

She didn't think twice. She released her grip on the bar and dropped the remaining few feet. Saber caught her in midair and turned, pulling her out of the dome just as Ace and Trig released the gate, trapping the beast inside while Sword engaged the heavy metal lock.

The loud shrieks of the Gartaian drew a shudder from Taylor. She wrapped her arms tightly around Saber's neck and buried her face against his shoulder. Her body was trembling uncontrollably from shock, fear, and adrenaline.

"That was amazing, Taylor," Lonnie whispered, staring at the Gartaian then at her.

"That was crazy," Trig muttered with a shake of his head. "Let's get out of here."

..*

Taylor sighed. Saber refused to put her down. She wasn't going to complain, at least not yet. At the moment, her body was still quivering from reaction. None of the men really talked. Cain and Ace led the way down the corridors to where the grate in the floor was located. Razor, then Hunter, went down first, followed by Sword and Thunder. After a few minutes, they came back and motioned for Trig to hand them Lonnie. Saber reluctantly set her on her feet before he dropped down through the hole. She watched him, worried when she saw his mouth tighten in pain.

Sitting down, she twisted and tried to drop down on her own, but he caught her around the waist and lowered her to the ground. She started to ask him if he was okay, but the look of warning in his eyes stopped her. Instead, she gripped his hand and stood to the side so that Dagger, Trig, Cain, and Ace could follow them.

She staggered when another blast shook the mountain. Saber wrapped his arm around her waist to steady her. With a nod to Razor to let him know that they were ready, the small group moved down the tunnel.

"The man with the purple eyes said to keep left at all times and it would lead to the base of the mountain. He told us to go east, that there was a rebel group in the mountains that would help us," Taylor whispered.

Saber squeezed her waist before slipping his hand down to grasp hers. She saw him finger the knife at his side. A small smile tugged at her lips. He was probably going to be doing that a lot for a while to make sure she hadn't taken it.

It took them a couple of hours to make their way through the maze of tunnels. The tunnel divided three times before they finally saw a small shaft of light coming from the end. Early morning light lit the circular entrance.

"Our skids should be just over the rise," Sword said, striding forward. "We came in through the upper level drainage. We didn't know there were two."

Thunder paused behind Sword, scanning the area. Taylor leaned back against the side wall next to Lonnie. She glanced down. The little boy was almost asleep. Bending, she sat down and pulled him into her arms. She didn't blame him. The last few weeks, sleep had been a luxury.

"We'll go get the skids," Thunder said. "We can use them to take you around to the others. Once we have them all, we can double up."

"Hunter and I can go for ours," Razor said with a shake of his head. "It isn't that far. Thunder, I want you and Sword to head out. There is a mining facility not far to the west. We need to know what kind of production is being done. This is more serious than we thought. Be careful. Get back to base as soon as you find out the information," he ordered before he turned to Trig. "Trig, you take Ace and Cain to get yours, Dagger, and Saber's skids. We'll meet back here. Dagger, you stay and help guard Taylor and the boy."

Dagger nodded, checking the charge on his rifle. "I'll scout the area. I haven't felt any tremors lately, maybe the fighter transports have finished," he said, gripping the weapon in his hand.

"Wait," Taylor muttered, gently laying Lonnie's head down. "Let me check your arm first. Do any of you have your emergency pack with you?"

A low curse escaped Saber and he rose to his feet. "Dagger's not the only one who needs medical attention," he said, propping his rifle against the wall and reaching into the pack at his waist. "He can take care of himself."

Dagger's eyes glittered with amusement. "Ah, Saber, your concern is touching," he chuckled.

"Remind me to kick your ass when we get out of this," Saber muttered, turning his back to Dagger and gently raising Taylor's arm. "Let me take a look at that cut."

Taylor rolled her eyes at Saber. The scratch on her arm was nothing compared to the nice long slit on Dagger's. She could see the fresh blood still seeping through the piece of torn shirt he had wrapped around it.

"His cut is worse than mine," she protested in a quiet voice.

"I don't think arguing with me at the moment is a good idea," Saber said, spraying the disinfectant with a numbing agent in it along the cut before running a thin laser to seal it. "I can't believe you did that. Do you have any idea how dangerous that little stunt was?"

"Don't forget her escape from the tower," Dagger pointed out as he replaced his own first aid kit.

Taylor shot Dagger a heated look. "Aren't you supposed to be scouting the area or something?" She snapped out in aggravation.

Dagger grinned and picked up his rifle. "As Jordan would say, I can feel the love," he replied with a soft chuckle. "I'll be back in a few minutes."

..*

Saber nodded, watching as Dagger disappeared out of the drainage tunnel. He returned his attention to Taylor when she swayed. He wrapped his arms around her and pulled her close to his body.

"I'm sorry," he whispered, resting his cheek against her head.

Taylor barely moved. He could feel her relax against him and couldn't help but savor the moment. It seemed like a lifetime since he had last held her like this.

"I didn't plan on any of this happening," she said with a sniff. "Achler… What he did to those people… To Ember."

Saber held Taylor, stroking her back in slow, calming strokes. If he ever wanted to know what it felt like to be powerless, it came when Taylor cried. These tears were different from the ones she had shed the day she had left. If he thought that it felt like his heart was being ripped out then, it hadn't changed. Each silent shudder tore at him.

"If I could wipe the memories from you, I would," Saber whispered. "Even a hardened warrior is not immune to the horrors of war. That you should see it so much in your life is unforgivable. It would seem that our presence has done nothing but bring you heartache and grief."

Taylor pulled back, a flash of stubborn anger on her face. Saber tenderly brushed her bruised face. He wished he had access to a full medical unit.

"Don't," she said with a shake of her head. "Jordan, Jesse, and I all made a deal to never think of the 'what might have been' or the 'what if's'. We promised we would just look ahead and make the best with what life gives us. Things happen for a reason. I would never have met you if your people hadn't come."

Saber turned his lips into the palm of her hand and pressed a kiss to the center of it. How he could have turned her away he would never understand. She was truly a gift from the Goddess and he came very close to throwing that gift away.

"I love you, Taylor Sampson," Saber groaned, threading his fingers into her hair.

Taylor tilted her head back and gazed up at him with a sly, watery smile. "Does this mean you accept my claim of you as my *Amate*?" She asked.

A soft chuckle escaped Saber and he nodded his head. "Yes, I accept your claim," he murmured before he sealed his lips over hers in a heated kiss that promised more to come.

"Saber," Dagger called as he entered the tunnel.

Saber broke the kiss and automatically reached for his rifle. Dagger was scowling as he stepped back into the shadows. A moment later, Sword and Thunder stepped inside. All three men had an expression of disgust on their faces.

"What is it?" Saber asked, glancing back and forth between the men.

"So much for rescuing the captives," Thunder said bitterly. "They took our skids."

"What about the others?" Saber asked, looking at Dagger.

"They are gone as well," Hunter said, stepping into the tunnel.

"I won't be surprised if ours are gone as well," Dagger said, turning and leaning against the wall so he could look out over the terrain. "Trig, Ace, and Cain should have been back by now if they had them."

Saber turned to look at Razor as he came back. "What about the fighter transports?" He asked, releasing Taylor when she stepped to the side and slid back down to the floor so she could cradle Lonnie's head. "Did you see any sign of them?"

"No," Razor replied with a shake of his head. "The fortress is pretty much leveled. They probably assumed no one survived, and if anyone did, they would be trapped beneath the rubble."

"I hear something," Hunter said, turning his head toward the entrance. He stepped closer to the opening so he could look out of the tunnel. "It's Trig, Ace, and Cain. They have the skids."

"Three are better than none," Razor said, stepping out as the men drew closer. "Did you see anything?" He asked, standing back as Trig, Ace, and Cain pulled up to the mouth of the tunnel and shut down the skids.

"Patrols to the south," Trig replied. "That's why it took us so long. We had to find cover as they scanned the area."

"Where are the other skids?" Cain asked, climbing off of one of the airbikes.

"Gone," Hunter replied in disgust. "The captives that escaped must have found them and taken them."

"Three skids can't carry everyone," Ace said, looking around.

"Do you think there could be anything in the fortress worth salvaging?" Taylor asked, looking up at the men. "Surely we could find something of use. Make a sled or something to pull behind them."

Hunter smiled down at Taylor. "You are just as smart and innovative as your sisters, you know that, right?" He teased.

Taylor grinned up at him. "Where do you think I learned it from?" She asked with a raised eyebrow.

"We didn't survive for four years on the streets without using our brains."

"No, you didn't," Hunter replied in a soft voice.

"We'll need something that we can pull behind them," Trig said with a frown.

"Or carry between them," Taylor suggested, biting her lip. "You don't want to leave any tracks. Maybe there is a way you can make a type of catamaran."

"Catamaran?" Saber asked with a puzzled frown.

Taylor nodded. "It was a type of boat that had a hull on each side and a canvas or a solid center between it. Those riding on it sat in the center."

"That makes sense," Saber replied, looking up at Hunter and Razor. "If what Trig said is true, that they have patrols out, the last thing we want is to leave a trail for them to follow."

"Sword, Thunder, Cain, and I can take a look in the fortress," Ace said, starting to turn when he heard Taylor release an expletive before she called his name.

"You're bleeding!" She told him, staring at the back of his leg.

Ace shrugged. "A minor wound, when we were running across the courtyard," he said.

"It still needs to be taken care of," Taylor insisted. "In this type of environment, it could become infected."

Ace's eyes crinkled at the corner. "I will attend to it once I step outside," he replied.

"Do you want me to take a look at it?" She asked in concern.

"NO!" Both Ace and Saber said at the same time.

Taylor frowned. "Why not? I deal with wounds all the time," she asked with a puzzled expression. "It doesn't look too bad, but it still needs to be taken care of just in case."

"He can take care of it himself," Saber informed her as he shot a warning glance at Ace.

"I don't want to destroy what's left of my clothing," Ace added with a lopsided grin. "It would be best to remove my trousers to seal the wound."

"Now that is a sight I would not want to see," Dagger retorted.

"Oh!" Taylor whispered as the realization of what he was saying sunk in. "Okay, well, if you need help, I'm here," she offered with a blush.

"I appreciate the offer, PT Taylor," Ace said with a bow of his head. "Come on. We will go see if there is anything we can salvage."

"We'll go with you," Razor said. "Everyone keep an eye out for patrols. Something tells me that the Waxians are going to realize that we aren't as easy to kill as they thought and will be coming back to make sure the job is finished."

Saber and Taylor watched as the other men left again. Saber moved over and sat down next to Taylor when he saw her shoulders droop. He would have to be blind to miss the dark shadows of exhaustion under her eyes.

"Is there any way to notify someone that we are here?" She asked in a tired voice.

Saber wrapped his arm around her and pulled her as close as he could without disturbing the boy in her lap. He leaned back and stared out at the bright morning light. Tilting his head, he rubbed his chin against her hair.

"No," he murmured. "This mission was not sanctioned by the rest of the council."

"Saber," Taylor whispered, closing her eyes and relaxing against him.

"Yes, my *Amate,*" Saber said in a gruff voice.

"I'm scared," she mumbled before a deep sigh escaped her and he knew she was asleep.

"So am I," Saber murmured, rubbing his chin back and forth against her hair. "I'm afraid of losing you," he added in a barely audible voice.

Chapter 19

Saber watched as Dagger carefully lifted Lonnie in his arms nearly three hours later. The sun was high in the sky. It was not the best time to be traveling, but they had little choice in the matter. Thunder and Sword had spotted troop movements in the South and reported that it looked like a patrol was coming to do a closer inspection of the fortress. They had managed to find a lone land transport. It was a small, two-seat vehicle used for low level patrols. Razor had ordered Thunder and Sword to leave immediately.

"We need the reconnaissance information," Razor said with a frown. "There is more to this than the Waxians wanting ore."

"Let's go. If we don't move now, we stand a good chance of being found," Hunter responded, studying Taylor's relaxed face. "She looks a lot like Leila when she is sleeping."

Saber carefully lifted Taylor up in his arms. She was so exhausted that she didn't even move. He stared down at her for a moment before he brushed a kiss across her forehead.

"She sleeps like her too when she is exhausted," Saber replied before his expression darkened. "How long before the patrols get here?"

"An hour," Hunter replied. "Achler appears convinced we didn't survive, otherwise they would have been here earlier."

Saber gave Hunter a sharp-toothed grin as he walked past him. "He'll realize his mistake when I kill him," he retorted.

"Who are you killing now?" Taylor asked sleepily, turning her face into his chest when the bright sun hit her face. "Ugh! Can someone please turn off the sun?"

The small group of men chuckled at her grumbling. She peeked out at Lonnie when she heard his giggle and winked. A smile curved Saber's lips. This was the Taylor he knew.

He carefully lowered her onto the makeshift floor of the air Catamaran they had constructed while she and Lonnie were sleeping. He would ride on it with Taylor and Lonnie. Each of the other men would double up, one operating the skid while the other provided coverage.

"Wow! This turned out pretty cool," Taylor said, rubbing her eyes before they widened. "My backpack!" She exclaimed excitedly. "Where did you find it?"

"I found it in the rubble," Hunter said with a smile. "I recognized it immediately from all the patches you have on it."

Taylor eagerly pulled it into her lap and unzipped it. Her fingers trembled as she pulled out the pictures she had stowed inside. Her fingers touched the cracked glass. It could be replaced. Fortunately, the picture of her, Jesse, Jordan, and their dad remained undamaged. Raising her eyes to Hunter, she gave him a watery smile.

"Thank you," she whispered.

Hunter's expression softened. "I'm glad that it was found," he said in a gruff voice before turning to Razor. "We had better be going. I want to put as much distance as possible between us and the patrol. Once Achler realizes we survived, he'll come looking for us."

"Where are we heading?" Taylor asked, repacking the picture.

"We will have to head north before we can curve around to the east. The Western faction has patrols all along the borders," he explained.

"But... That's the way the other captives were heading," she said in concern. "The guy with the purple eyes told them to head to the mountains of the Crescent Moon."

"They know the Western sector well enough to know how to avoid them," Hunter said with a shrug. "If they don't, there is not much we can do about it."

Taylor sighed. "Being a soldier sucks," she muttered, clutching her backpack to her chest.

Saber touched the bruise on her chin. "There is never a good side to war. Many innocent people are the ones who truly suffer," he murmured. "A true soldier does what he can to protect them."

Taylor rubbed her cheek against his hand before sitting back as the skids moved forward. It was a little jerky at first as the men tested the best speed and distance apart to travel to keep the items they had salvaged and Taylor, Saber, and Lonnie from flying off. Saber quietly explained that they built a frame with supports before covering it with a large tarp and attaching it to the three remaining skids.

"Your idea was brilliant," he said. "We were able to bring additional weapons, as well as essential survival equipment like food and water that the others salvaged."

Taylor shook her head. "You're right, I am brilliant," she teased. "I would have thought of the food and water before the weapons."

Saber's expression sobered. "Weapons can be just as much as a necessity, Taylor. This is a lawless land. Without a way to protect yourself, food and water will do little to save you."

Taylor sighed and looked at Lonnie. Saber turned his head, following where she was looking. Her face was so expressive. He could sit and watch the different emotions dance across her face all day.

He saw that she was staring at the boy. Lonnie was leaning against a box staring out at the desert. The boy looked so young. He couldn't remember being that young. He turned his gaze back to Taylor. Both she and Lonnie's lives had been torn apart when they were just beginning. At least he had known a stable home life, where he could be young before he began his training.

He reached over and ran his finger along her hand, smiling when she immediately turned it over so she could wind her fingers through his. A satisfied smile curved his lips. He had been such an idiot the past five years.

"How is your leg?" She asked, tightening her fingers around his as if afraid her question would cause him to pull away from her.

"Stiff," he admitted. "I went to the healer the day I found out about your disappearance."

Taylor looked up at him. "What did he say?" She asked with a slight tremble in her voice.

Saber sighed and looked down at her briefly before returning his gaze to the desolate landscape. His right hand moved down to rub his leg. He squeezed her fingers.

"I should have talked to you," he admitted. "The bone wasn't healing correctly. Too much of it had been shattered. The first healers who attended to me were able to clean most of the fragment out and repair some of the damage done. I wasn't able to do much physical therapy due to the bone not healing, and the area around it continued to fracture."

Taylor nodded. "I'm surprised they didn't amputate your leg. I saw the scans. I'm not a healer, but I could see the extent of the damage. The nerves and muscles were in bad shape, too," she said. "After your third surgery, the healer highly recommended removing it and fitting you with a robotic leg, but you refused."

"How did you see the scans?" Saber asked, scowling down at her. "Are you telling me that you've known all along what has been happening?"

"Of course," she replied with a sigh. "I had Jordan hack into your medical records. Every time any updates were done, I was sent a copy of it."

A grumble of disbelief escaped him. "Why didn't you tell me?" He demanded, shaking his head.

Taylor chuckled before she leaned over to brush a kiss to his lips. "Because I knew that you would probably have stopped going to the healer. You can be very hard-headed when you get your mind stuck on something. I was afraid if you knew, you wouldn't let me come over anymore. I followed along with the recommended therapy from the healers. It was important to keep your other muscles strong. With the damage to your leg, it would throw off your posture and would affect the rest of your body," she explained.

"And if it was necessary…," he paused and drew in a deep breath before continuing. "What would you have done if they had decided to take my leg?"

Taylor leaned into him. "Love you, help you, be there for you, and love you some more," she replied.

"Shewta!" Saber whispered, shaking his head. "You must truly love me to have put up with everything I put you through."

Taylor chuckled. "Yeah, well, payback is a bitch and I think she had puppies in your case. I still remember your comment the day I left. I've had plenty of time to think of how you can grovel. I've come up with a ton of really good ideas," she remarked with a teasing smile. "Is there any water?"

"Yes, in the bag to your left. Get one for Lonnie, as well," Saber replied. "The heat will dehydrate you both more than it will us."

"Show off," Taylor teased before turning on her hands and knees to reach for the bag.

A low rumble escaped Saber as his gaze swept over the curve of Taylor's ass. He turned when he felt another set of eyes on them. Ace's gaze was glued to Taylor as well. He shot the other male a look of warning.

"She's mine," Saber snarled.

Ace raised an eyebrow and looked at Saber's wrists before he glanced over at Taylor. "I don't see your mark on her," he replied.

Saber's hand moved to the rifle at his side. "She's mine," he repeated. "Do not challenge me, Ace. I will kill for her."

Ace didn't reply. His gaze flickered to where Taylor was sitting next to the boy. Saber watched the male until he returned his attention back to the landscape. Pulling down his MMOS, he zoomed into the distance. Over the fortress, he could barely make out a fighter transport firing down into the structure. It would appear Achler decided he didn't want to take any chances.

..*

Prymorus Achler leaned back in his chair and stared moodily at the holographic map. In the background, he could hear several men talking, including the Kassisan that had been 'assigned' to him. He didn't trust the bastard. He fingered his drink as he thought about what had happened during the night.

The Kassisan had saved his life, but if he expected any special consideration or appreciation for that fact, he was in the wrong company. The Waxians were mercenaries. They liked to kill and they liked to make money. Most of the time, they did it for both, but on a few rare occasions, they did it for pleasure. The one thing they never did was keep a dangerous enemy for too long.

Cordus Kelman had done that. The Drethulans had hired a dozen Waxian warlords to do two things: deliver enough weapons to destroy the Alliance forces and discover the Trivator's weakness. Kelman's detailed records of the Trivator he used in the fight rings had shown them that when it came to fighting – and surviving – the warrior species were second to none. The fact that Kelman's experiment earned him a fortune was proof of that.

He had been doubtful when the other Waxian told him about his plans. Capture several Trivators and use them in the fight ring to observe how they fought, what their endurance and pain level tolerance were, and how long they could keep fighting.

Prymorus had an idea that the Trivator would still be making Kelman credits if the bastard hadn't killed him. The only good thing that came out of Kelman's experiment was finally finding the Trivators' one weakness… their females. The Trivators might protect those that are weaker, but as Razor had proven, they could also look the other way if it meant destroying an enemy – except when it came to a female that was under their protection.

Which meant a mated Trivator would do anything for his female, including not attacking those that held her as a prisoner for fear of harming her, Prymorus thought, playing with the knife as he continued to study the map.

"You appear deep in thought," the Kassisan commented, walking toward the table where Prymorus was sitting.

A flash of anger went through him when the huge bastard placed a bottle of his most expensive liquor down on the table and poured two glasses. He watched suspiciously as the man pushed a glass in front of him before sitting down in the chair facing him. His gaze was drawn to the man's hands.

"I don't remember inviting you to partake of my best liquor, Dakar," Prymorus snapped, leaning forward to snatch the bottle from across the table.

Dakar chuckled, fingering the glass before slowly raising it to his lips and taking a sip. Prymorus watched as the Kassisan seemed to savor it before swallowing. A small part of him wished the fiery liquor would burn a hole through the man's chest.

"It is too good to waste sitting in a bottle and growing stale," Dakar replied with a shrug. "The fighter transports destroyed the fortress, why waste time and resources on returning there?"

Prymorus turned his gaze back to the map. "I've sent a patrol to make sure that nothing survived. I don't want to take a chance of any of those Trivator warriors making it out," he growl in frustration. "The girl was key to my plans. She is under the protection of two of the most powerful Trivators in the Alliance."

"Did you ever find out how she escaped?" Dakar asked, looking at the fortress. "It is a long way from the tower to the lower catacombs where the other prisoners were being held."

Prymorus' gaze narrowed and he shook his head. "I was too busy trying to kill those Trivator bastards to investigate. It seems strange that they missed you as you were wandering around the fortress. They killed many of my men before the alarm was sounded, but somehow passed you by," he observed.

Dakar simply raised his drink and took a sip. The man was too cool, too controlled, and too lucky for Prymorus' taste. Dakar had departed *The Hole* on the Bruttus Spaceport in the Tessalon galaxy shortly before the Drethulan, Jolin Talja, was killed. A group of Trivators had arrived to rescue the other caged warrior.

Last night, Dakar had appeared out of the shadows and pushed him out of the line of fire that would have killed him. What bothered him was that he had seen the Kassisan in action. He never missed his target, yet last night he had missed every time he aimed at one of the Trivator warriors.

"I've sent a patrol back to the fortress to make sure there were no survivors," Prymorus added, sipping his drink. "I've also ordered increased patrols along the border. We need to harvest as much ore as possible."

"Production is at full capacity," Dakar replied with a raised eyebrow. "The workers are already stretched as far as they can go."

"Extend their shifts," Prymorus ordered, staring at Dakar over the rim of his glass. "I also have a mission for you." Dakar's lips tightened, but he didn't say anything. "I want you to kidnap the Trivator Councilman's woman."

Distaste flashed across Dakar's face and a bored expression settled over it. Prymorus watched in amusement. He was curious to see how lucky the Kassisan was at infiltrating the Trivator forces. He was also testing the Kassisan. The male was always arguing with him about the mine workers.

"I believe you killed her when you blew up the fortress," Dakar finally said with a wave of his hand to the hologram. "That might be a rather messy mission."

Prymorus sat back in his chair. "Not that one, she was not his woman, merely one under his protection. I want you to kidnap Razor's female."

Dakar grimaced. "It would be better to kill me now," he replied dryly. "How do you propose I kidnap this woman? If I remember correctly from the reports, the last time someone tried to kidnap a Trivator's woman, it ended badly – for the Waxian stupid enough to try it. What is the use anyway? Both Razor and Hunter are dead. The fortress, remember?"

Prymorus' lips tightened. "Are you refusing?" He asked in a quiet tone that held a hint of malice in it.

Dakar released a deep sigh. "The Drethulans hired me to make sure you Waxians were following through with their end of the agreement. I do not work for you or any other member of the Waxian forces. The fact that I saved your ass last night was beyond my normal job guidelines. I simply did it so that production of the needed ore would not be delayed. Do not attempt to order me around, Waxian. Your species aren't the only ones who enjoy killing."

Prymorus placed his empty glass on the table and stood up, his hand moved to his side where he kept his laser pistol. His focus remained glued on the steely-eyed male still sitting across from him. His fingers moved to his waist, but paused. Sweat beaded on his brow. The Kassisan was too confident, and a feeling that he was suddenly in mortal danger washed through him. His hand relaxed back down to his side.

"Be careful who you threaten, Kassisan," Prymorus growled in a soft tone. "The Drethulans can always replace you."

Dakar casually rose out of his seat, his own blaster in his hand. The smug smile on his face was not reflected in his eyes. Prymorus' fists clenched by his side; he had been right. The bastard probably had his weapon trained on him the entire time.

"All of us are expendable," Dakar replied, not bothering to sheath his weapon. "I suggest you not forget that, as well, Achler. The Drethulans are expecting an update."

Prymorus watched as Dakar's gaze flickered to the hologram image of the fortress once more before he stepped away from the table. The Kassisan didn't turn all the way until he could step out of the room. Prymorus leaned forward, placing his hands on the table in front of him in aggravation. He angrily stared at the map.

"I want a report from the patrol," he ordered, turning his attention to one of the men directing movements at the communication console. "Tell them to sift through the rubble until they find every single one of the Trivators' bodies."

"Yes, sir," the man replied, turning and conveying the message to the patrol team.

Chapter 20

Taylor handed a nutrition pack to Lonnie. She smiled down at the boy. He returned her smile, but it quickly sagged in the intense heat.

"It will cool off in a couple of hours," she murmured.

"I know," Lonnie replied.

She picked up several of the drink packs and carried them to where the men were standing, looking off into the horizon. Her eyes swept over Saber's tall form. Pleasure and pride washed through her. A rosy blush that had nothing to do with the heat suffused her cheeks when he turned and watched as she struggled to climb the small sand dune.

"I know you guys are big, tough warriors, but I also know that dehydration doesn't care about that," she said, smiling up at them.

"Thank you, Taylor," Hunter replied, reaching for one of the packs.

"What's wrong?" She asked, sensing the tension in the air.

Saber nodded to the horizon. Taylor turned to see what he was looking at. Her eyes widened when she saw the thick, black sky. She had been on the planet long enough to know what it was – one of their intense storms. There had been a half dozen of them in the last six months. The worst ones happened in the Western region, but the East was not immune to them.

"Oh, shit!" Taylor breathed out. "That's a whole lot of sand."

Ace chuckled, reaching for one of the water packs. "Yes, it is," he replied, ignoring the low growl of warning from Saber.

Taylor wrinkled her nose at Saber. "So, what are we going to do?" She asked with a worried frown as she handed the rest of the men their packs. "It's too dangerous to remain outside. The sand will slice through us."

"There's a cut in the sandstone," Razor said, focusing in on the area. "Hopefully there will be a cavern cut out in the rock face. The nomads in the area use them."

"Can we make it in time? What about the skids? I thought they needed to cool off," she said, turning to look at Saber.

Saber's grim expression was enough of an answer. They didn't have a choice. If they didn't make it, they would die. Turning, she jerked to a stop when she saw a line of dust rising in the distance in the direction they had come.

"Saber," Taylor whispered, staring in horror.

She vaguely heard the men's soft curses. They were trapped; in front of them, the massive sandstorm; behind them, the patrol.

"Let's go," Saber growled, grabbing Taylor's hand and pulling her back toward the skids.

She half ran, half slid down the slope of sand to the bottom. Her gaze swept the area, focusing on Lonnie, who was lying in the shade under the catamaran. He crawled out when he saw them running toward the skids.

"What is it, PT Taylor?" He asked in a frightened voice.

"We've got to go, sweetheart," Taylor replied in an urgent voice, releasing Saber's hand so she could help Lonnie back onto the skids.

Lonnie looked around confused and frightened. "I thought the machines needed to cool," he said.

"They should be cool enough to get us where we need to go," Saber replied, turning and sitting down on the edge.

"Go!" Hunter shouted.

Taylor glanced around at the determined faces. Her lips curved into a nervous smile when she saw Dagger wink at her. She wrapped her arm tightly around Lonnie and held him when the skids jerked forward. Her eyes remained glued to the patrol moving rapidly across the desert floor until the skids passed over the dune.

The landscape began to change. This area was more sand and less rock. It would make the journey more difficult. A half hour into their race across the dunes, Taylor almost lost her balance when the skid Cain was operating jerked and died. The sudden loss of power caused the catamaran to tilt to the left.

"Stop!" Cain yelled.

Razor turned, nodding when Hunter spoke to him. Dagger glanced over and shut down his skid. Saber jumped off the catamaran before turning to help Taylor and Lonnie.

Taylor shielded her eyes from the spray of sand that was kicked up by the growing storm. She stepped closer to Saber so she could hear what was being said.

"The engine's gone," Ace was saying in disgust. "Between the heat, sand, and weight, we are lucky we got this far."

Trig looked off in the distance with a grim expression. "There's no way we'll make the canyon."

"What about the other two skids?" Saber asked.

Dagger shook his head. "Mine was overheating," he admitted. "We'd have been lucky if it made it to the next rise."

Taylor saw Saber glance down at her. His mouth tightened into a straight line as he looked behind them, then at the storm. Her hand instinctively reached for his.

"Razor, what about your skid?" Saber asked.

Razor's turned his gaze to Taylor and Lonnie. Taylor's head was already shaking when she saw the intense focus reflected in them. She knew what he was going to say.

"No," she whispered, her throat tight with fear. "No, I won't leave you guys here."

"It will get Taylor and Lonnie to the canyon," Razor replied in a calm voice. "We'll pack enough nutrition packs to last her and the boy several days."

"No," Taylor said again, turning to Saber. Her eyes filled with tears. "No! I'm not leaving you guys here."

Saber turned to her and gripped her arms. "You have to," he murmured in a soft voice. "Think about Lonnie, Taylor. You have to get him to safety."

"What about you?" She asked, brushing an irritated hand over her cheek. "If I take the only working skid, there is no way you or the others will survive."

"The Mountains of the Crescent Moon are on the other side of the storm," Saber said. "Get to the canyon. We'll ride out the storm here. Once it is over, I want you to make for the mountain. We'll catch up with you."

Taylor shook her head again. "You have the storm in front of you and the patrol behind you, how are you going to make it through that?" She asked stubbornly.

"Think of the boy," Saber repeated, glancing at where Lonnie stood watching them.

"I just got you back," Taylor whispered, staring up at Saber. "I swear, if you don't come, I'm going to come looking for you…" She paused and looked at the other men. "I'll come looking for all of you. Jesse, Jordan, and Kali would kick my ass if I didn't."

"Go, Taylor," Hunter said, stepping up to her. "Jesse knows I will do everything I can to return to her."

"Just as Jordan does," Dagger said with a grin.

"And Kali," Razor reluctantly admitted with a smile.

"I hate to be the bearer of bad news, but if she is going to make it, she and the boy need to get going," Trig said in a grim voice. "It looks like the storm and the patrol are both determined to find us first."

Taylor released a shaky breath and looked over to where Ace and Cain were unhooking the skids from the catamaran. Trig grabbed a box of nutrition packs and attached it to the back with some of the straps. Razor had picked Lonnie up and was carrying him over to the skid.

"Here, wear these," Saber ordered, pulling his goggles off. "The cut in the canyon is programmed into it, as well as the base of the mountains. Find shelter and cover up until the storm passes. We'll come to you on the other side of the border."

Taylor reluctantly reached for the goggles. She glanced up at Saber before throwing her arms around his neck and pressing a hot, demanding kiss to his lips. Sliding her hands back down his chest, she stepped back and stared at him for a moment before turning and climbing on the skid.

"Be safe," he ordered, staring at her like a dying man staring at a pool of water that was just out of his reach. "I love you, my *Amate*. I will come for you."

"You better," she retorted in a thick voice.

Her eyes glistened with tears. Reaching up, she pulled the goggles down to hide how much leaving him behind was killing her. Pressing the start button, she felt the skid power up. She twisted the handgrip and pressed down on the foot pads, gliding away from the men. She glanced at the rearview screen. The men were already preparing for the battle for their lives.

***

Taylor's gaze flickered back and forth between the destination ahead of her, the storm, and the temperature readings of the skid. Without the extra weight, the skid was staying within the upper level of the normal range. She could feel Lonnie gripping her tightly around the waist, his head buried against her to protect it from the blowing sand.

She had slipped on extra clothing and wrapped a scarf around her head. She had done the same to Lonnie, but the sand still found a way inside her clothing. It also found the small areas of skin. The small granules stung when they struck.

Her heart lifted to her throat when the skid flew up the side of a dune and was airborne for a moment before it slid down the other side. She pressed the accelerator down as the wind grew worse. It was almost impossible to see now. She was forced to use the digital readout in the goggles. Turning to the left, she could see the entrance to the canyon up ahead.

The skid flew into the narrow passage just as a massive wave of sand rolled over, darkening the day to night. She could feel Lonnie's arms trembling against her as she leaned from side to side. A cry of relief escaped her when she spotted one of the narrow caves that littered the canyons to the right.

She released her grip on the accelerator and tilted her feet back, slowly applying the brakes. Swinging the skid around, she ducked as she passed under the overhang and into the dark, cool cave. The goggles immediately switched to night mode, so she could look around her as she drew the skid to a stop.

It was barren, with a few piles of sand that had blown in along one edge. Shutting down the skid, she felt Lonnie release her waist so she could slide off the airbike. She reached into the front compartment and pulled out a torch. Twisting it, she pulled off the goggles and held up the glowing rod.

"It's okay," she whispered, her voice echoing in the shallow cavern.

Lonnie blinked and looked around. "Why doesn't the sand blow in here?" He asked, sliding off the skid and coming to stand next to her.

Taylor glanced outside. Sheets of sand were blowing down the canyon, but the way the sandstone had cut into the walls, it had created a lip that steered the wind and sand away from the opening. Nature was a wondrous thing, no matter what planet a person was on, she couldn't help but think.

"It's just the way nature works," she replied. "Let's push the bike to the back of the cave. We'll need the tarp to help keep us warm. I can feel the temperature dropping already."

"Me, too," Lonnie said with a sigh as he helped push on the back of the skid. "Do you think the warriors will be alright, PT Taylor?" He asked in a soft voice.

"Yes," she responded.

She didn't say anything else. She couldn't at the moment. Just the thought of Saber and the others out there was enough to make her want to scream. She didn't think her running around like a Dodo bird out in the middle of an alien sandstorm would help the situation.

"Come on, let's get the nutrition packs out and see what we've got," she murmured. "Are you hungry?"

"No," Lonnie said, kicking the dirt. "I really miss my mom and dad."

"I know," she said, squeezing his shoulder. "I still miss mine."

"Are your parents on your planet?" Lonnie asked, picking up several packs and carrying them over to Taylor.

"You could say that," she murmured. "My mom died when I was still a baby. My dad…." Her throat tightened again as she thought of him. Shaking her head, she forced away the sad thoughts. "My dad worked as a policeman. He was killed the first day the Trivator forces came to our world. It was just my two older sisters and me until Saber, Hunter, and Dagger found us." She paused again and grinned. "Actually, it was my older sister, Jesse, who found Hunter. She saved him from a group of really nasty humans."

"Just like you saved me," Lonnie replied with a grin.

"Yeah, just like I saved you," Taylor responded.

Three hours later, Taylor stared out of the cave at the sandstorm. It was still blowing like crazy. She had found some old driftwood that had washed down during the days when rain fell in the area and had stacked it together to make a fire.

She and Lonnie had curled up inside the tarp next to it. Lonnie had finally fallen asleep just a few minutes before. She leaned back against the wall of the cave. She reached over and pulled her backpack closer to her. Reaching inside, she pulled out the small notebook and pen. She knew it was old fashioned, but there was something special about writing things down.

Biting the tip of the pen, she smiled. She refused to believe the guys wouldn't make it. Her gaze flickered to the blasting sand and her lips tightened in determination. She knew Saber, Hunter, Razor, Dagger, and Trig. Those five guys were not only resourceful, they were smart and had tons of training. They were a combination of MacGyver and 007 all rolled into one.

She opened her notebook to the page she had started the night she left, three months ago. At the top of the page, she had written Saber's name and drawn all kinds of little doodles around it. She had been pretty pissed that night and there were a lot of flames around his name. Glancing down, she studied her list of things he could do to make up for being such a shit.

1. *He accepts that I love him unconditionally, but that I won't be walked on. A yellow ribbon on the tree out front will tell me that he accepts that. If he doesn't… I need to let him go.*
2. *A dozen yellow roses, or equivalent alien flower, every day for a year.*
3. *Him on one knee telling me he loves me.*
4. *Ties, for him, so I can tie him down and have my way with him until he confesses he loves me forever and beyond.*
5. *Me on top.*
6. *Me on top.*
7. *Me on top. P.S. I like being on top.*
8. *Okay, him on top.*

9. *Love-making in the bathroom.*
10. *Love-making in the kitchen.*
11. *Love-making in the garden.*
12. *Love-making in the den.*
13. *Him, accepting he is my Amate.*
14. *Go airbiking together.*
15. *Making love in every room of the house all in the same day, okay, week. I might not be able to walk if it was the same day.*

Taylor sighed. She doodled hearts around the page with her and Saber's name on it. The list went on and on. Her hand shook as she reached down and added one last item to the list before she closed the notebook and set it aside.

She blinked sleepily and slid down next to Lonnie. She wrapped her arm around him, just like Jordan and Jesse used to do to her. Drawing in a deep breath, she released it and relaxed. Her life was so different from anything that she could ever have imagined.

"I love you, Saber," she whispered in the dim light. "I hope you can feel it."

Her eyelids fluttered closed with exhaustion. A smile curved her lips as she remembered Saber's kiss. He was going to come to her. His kiss had told her that he wouldn't stop until they were together again.

Chapter 21

Saber strained as he pushed up. Each man slowly emerged from the sand like ghost crabs on the beach, clawing and wiggling out from under the catamaran. He shook the sand from his hair before he slid out from under the taut, sand-covered tarp. He paused, listening before murmuring to the others that it was clear.

It was just before dawn and a hint of the sun could be seen on the horizon. Saber nodded to the other men. They spread out, each searching for the patrol that had been heading their way.

Saber topped a newly formed slope of sand and dropped down to lie along the rim. Less than a kilometer away were the remains of the patrol. He waited for several minutes, trying to see if there were any survivors.

He turned his head when he felt Trig and Dagger slip down beside him. Trig slid his goggles on and focused. He was silent a moment before he muttered a curse.

"I see at least three survivors," he said with a shake of his head. "We could take them out, but I imagine they have already called for assistance."

"That is all the more reason to eliminate them. We need to get to the canyon," Saber said, sliding down the sand before turning.

A few minutes later, they were retracing their steps up the slope. Saber nodded when Trig raised three fingers. Focusing, they worked in sync, picking off each member of the patrol that had survived. Rising up, they approached the small cluster of transports. The air transport had turned around. They knew their airships were no match for the storm.

Walking among the dead, Saber could see that most of the men were Waxians. They should have listened to the three survivors. They must be members of the Western resistance.

"These guys look just as bad dead as they do when they are alive," Ace commented, examining the almost skeletal remains of the Waxian where the sand had sliced through the flesh and tissue.

"This one, too," Cain called out.

Razor and Hunter searched the remains of the other ground transport. Saber walked through the camp, pausing by the men they had just killed. He pulled the cover from one man's face. A curse escaped him and he fell back when the creature suddenly turned on him.

"Drethulans!" He shouted, scrambling backwards and pulling his rifle around.

Saber fired at the creature as it began to shake and expand. Several large holes appeared in the tentacles that expanded outward from his assault. He fired again before it pushed down and disappeared under the sand.

Rolling to his feet, he heard the others firing on the other two creatures. He moved, turning in a circle when he felt the sand under his feet shift. His gaze narrowed, following the slight movement of the granules.

He flipped the switch on his rifle to full power. Stepping to the side, he followed the movement in slow, measured steps in an effort to minimize the impact of his weight on the sand so the Drethulan couldn't tell where he was. Saber's eyes froze on the sand two feet away from him.

He rolled to the side as the sand exploded outward, showering him in its stinging rain. He waited until the Drethulan's mouth opened to reveal hundreds of razor-sharp teeth. Saber rose up on one knee and aimed for the center of the twisting teeth.

"I don't think so, you ugly bastard," Saber growled, firing a series of shots into the Drethulan's mouth that was coming toward him.

Saber rose to his feet and twisted around when he heard laser fire. He ran forward, jumping up onto the front of one of the transports and firing on the Drethulan that had come up behind Cain while he was firing at the third one.

"Cain, look out!" Ace shouted.

Cain turned, and his face suddenly paled with a look of shock as one of the Drethulan's long tentacles pierced his chest. He stumbled backwards, firing on the creature, even as his knees gave out. Saber swung off the transport, firing point blank into the Drethulan's limb.

He ignored the Drethulans as he raced forward to catch Cain as he fell backwards. Regret pierced Saber when he saw the Trivator's head roll to the side. His eyes stared blankly outward over the barren dunes. He carefully lowered Cain down to the sand and turned.

"Cain?" Ace asked, running over.

Saber shook his head. "The Drethulans?" He asked.

"Dead. We checked the others. The rest were Waxians," Dagger replied, staring down with regret at Cain's lifeless body.

"*Shewta*!" Razor exclaimed when he saw Cain.

"He had no family," Ace said in a quiet voice, staring up at the sky. "Perhaps in the next life he will be given one for his loyalty and sacrifice."

Saber nodded, looking at Hunter and Trig. "Did you find anything?" He asked.

Trig nodded. "I found a working transport. Not in the best shape, but it started," he replied, glancing down at Cain.

"Ace said he had no family," Saber replied, answering Trig's unspoken question.

Trig nodded. Each man made sure their laser rifle was at full charge. Stepping back, they aimed it at Cain's body. Razor gave the quiet command to fire. Within seconds, the fine ash of Cain's remains mixed with the sands of the desert.

Turning, Saber stared down at his wrists. A wave of pain flashed through him when he thought again of the gift he had been given and how close he had come to throwing it away. A family was the greatest honor a Trivator warrior could be given. The urge to rejoin Taylor and sweep her away to the safety of his home on Rathon gave Saber a renewed determination to make Taylor his *Amate* as soon as possible.

* * *

Taylor slowly came awake. She was amazed that she had slept so well considering everything that had happened. She blinked in surprise when she saw a pair of glowing amber eyes staring back at her. A soft, unexplained giggle escaped her. She knew she should be terrified, but it was hard to be when all she could see was her dirty face reflected back at her.

"Man, I need a bath," she said in a voice husky from sleep. "I'm surprised you aren't running screaming. I swear, I've got sand in places where no sand should ever be."

A slender hand reached up and removed the helmet, revealing the face of a young woman. She stared at Taylor before her eyes moved down to Lonnie. Taylor grabbed the woman's hand when she started to touch him.

"He's under my protection," Taylor said with a pointed look before she released the strange woman's wrist. "I just want you to know that."

The woman turned her gaze back to Taylor. "You are either very brave or very stupid," the woman responded, rising to her feet. "Bring her and Londius."

"PT Taylor," Lonnie mumbled sleepily as he sat up. "What's wrong?"

"How did you know his name?" Taylor demanded, rising to her feet when two helmet-clad men stepped forward.

"Maridi!" Lonnie exclaimed, rolling to his feet with a laugh.

Maridi chuckled as she wrapped her arms around Lonnie. Taylor watched the exchange, feeling very confused. Tucking her messy hair behind her ear, she folded her arms across her chest and scowled at the two embracing figures.

"Ah, Lonnie, who is this?" Taylor asked, raising her eyebrow at the girl that wasn't much older than she was. "She looks familiar."

"She should," Lonnie replied with a huge grin. "This is my sister, Maridi."

"Maridi?" Taylor said, rubbing her forehead. "But, I thought your family lived in the Eastern section."

"That is what we wanted you to think," Maridi said. "Come, our father and mother will be very pleased that my brother has returned."

"I bet," Taylor mumbled, hurriedly reaching down to grab her backpack. "What about the other stuff?"

"It is safe," Maridi replied with a wave of her hand. "Come, we must move before the air patrols cross."

Taylor stumbled out into the bright morning light. She blinked several times to clear her vision before she could focus on where she was going. This is one of those mornings when anything with a lot of caffeine might have come in handy. She felt like she had fog for brains at the moment.

"Ah, Maridi," Taylor called out. "Where are we going? I need to be heading to the mountains."

"I know," Maridi replied as she picked up her pace.

Taylor grimaced. The girl was really beginning to piss her off. She would have just told her to go on if it hadn't been for the two guys behind her with the long poles that looked suspiciously like they could light up her ass if she wasn't careful.

Focusing on her breathing, she decided the best thing to do was make sure that Lonnie was safe, then see if she could steal some kind of transport and go find Saber and the others. A wave of guilt flooded her for a second when she realized that all her thoughts had been on Saber, not Hunter, Dagger, or Razor. Jesse, Jordan, and Kali would kill her if their men didn't make it back. Knowing how she felt about Saber, she could understand why.

Taylor slowed when she saw Maridi start up a long row of stairs. She stopped and blinked up in awe. At the end of the winding canyon was a monument of some kind. Huge statues stood like silent sentinels staring down at her.

"Back off," Taylor muttered when one of the men touched her with the end of the rod. "This is like – incredible. You can at least give me a second to appreciate it."

"Come, PT Taylor, my parents are expecting you," Maridi called down with a grin.

"It's just Taylor," Taylor replied as she stepped up to the sand-colored staircase.

Carefully climbing up the staircase, Taylor felt like she had just jumped from one movie set to another. She shook her head. Saber was never going to believe this! She paused at the entrance to look down the canyon.

The tall walls concealed most of the structure. The only thing she could see was the narrowed area at the very end where bright sunlight shown down into the canyon. Swallowing, she cast an annoyed glance at the guards behind her before she turned and stepped through the massive stone entrance.

Chapter 22

Western Region Council Offices:
Prymorus stood at the window of the office he had taken over in the Western Council. He had sent the Kassisan on a mission to check the ore productions at one of the remote mines. He didn't care that the man had proven himself to the Drethulan warlord that was overseeing this project. The bastard had saved his life as well, but that didn't mean he trusted him.

He turned when he heard the knock at his office door. Calling out a command for the person to enter, he stared coldly at the young officer that he had instructed to retrieve information on the bodies of the Trivators.

"Well?" He demanded.

The Disesian looked just over his shoulder when he responded. Prymorus knew the male was terrified. He could smell it, but he remained standing at attention.

"Nothing, sir," the Disesian replied. "The patrol reported that there were no remains of Trivators in the rubble. The report stated that the area appeared to have been pillaged. One of the hunters followed the tracks back to an underground drainage on the northeast side of the mountain. A second patrol discovered a number of captives trying to escape across the desert to the mountains and opened fire. The sole survivor stated before she was killed that the group had escaped from the lower catacombs of the fortress."

Prymorus' features twisted in rage at the knowledge that the Trivators had escaped. His fists clenched. Striding over to his desk, he pulled up a map of the area.

"Where is the patrol now?" He asked in a harsh voice.

"They… They are dead, sir," the male said. "The second patrol found them. It appears most of the men were killed during a sandstorm."

Prymorus' head jerked up and his eyes narrowed. "Most?" He repeated.

The male looked away. "Yes, sir," he replied in a quiet voice. "The three Drethulans with the patrol were killed by laser fire."

"Get me the Kassisan, Dakar," Prymorus ordered, sitting down at his desk.

Prymorus looked up when the male didn't immediately reply. His mouth tightened as he pulled up a message that had been waiting for him. The message was from three hours ago. He had heard it come in, but had ignored it. Pressing the control, he saw Dakar's standard signature.

I told you that I don't take orders from you. Our work service has been voided.

Rage pulled Prymorus out of his chair again. "Shut down all departures. I want that Kassisan's head on my desk," he growled.

"He… He has already left the planet, sir," the male stuttered.

Prymorus walked around the desk with slow, purposeful steps, like a huge predator stalking its prey. A vicious smile curved his lips as he stared at the young Disesian with piercing black eyes. His hand moved to his hip.

"Then, I guess your head will have to do," he snarled, raising his laser sword.

..*

An hour later, Prymorus stepped out of the cleaning unit in his office. He ran the towel over his bald head as he walked by his bloodstained desk. Tossing the towel to the side, he poured himself a glass of his favorite liquor. He had only taken a couple of sips of it when the computer on his desk chimed.

Turning, he walked over to it and sat down, staring moodily at the computer before he leaned forward and pressed in his code. A message from his client immediately came up. He read the message through twice before he leaned back in his chair. Lifting the glass in his hand to his mouth, he quickly swallowed down the contents before ordering one of the guards to enter.

"Yes, sir," the guard said, not looking at the desk.

"Have my warship prepared for immediate departure," Prymorus ordered.

"Yes, sir," the guard said with a bow of his head.

Prymorus waited until the door shut behind the guard before he turned to stare into the empty eyes of the young officer. A calculating gleam came into them.

A Trivator values one thing above all else – his female, he thought. Bending, he stared into the sightless eyes.

"I wonder if the Kassisan does, as well?" he murmured. "Just think – a new planet to destroy and perhaps a mate or two to go with it. What could be better revenge than that?" He asked as he reached out and closed the male's eyes. "Yes, I thought you would agree with me."

***

"Hold up," Saber called down as the transport glided to a stop just outside the canyon.

"What is it?" Razor asked, staring straight ahead.

"Trig, scan for detection systems," Saber ordered.

"What is it?" Hunter asked in a quiet voice, standing up in the back next to Saber.

"For just a second, I had a reading," Saber murmured. "My gut is telling me to check it out."

Hunter leaned over and tapped Razor on the shoulder. He waved his hand across his throat for Razor to turn off the transport. Saber, Dagger, Trig, Ace, and Hunter climbed out of the transport.

"Spread out," Saber ordered. "Look for a low pulse system."

They spread out, not crossing into the canyon, but surveying the outer area. A low curse escaped Saber when he caught another glimpse of the pulse, but lost it before he could capture the frequency. It was an antiquated, but effective security system.

"I've got it," Hunter called out. "Switch down to two point one seven."

Saber nodded, adjusting the detection system on his goggles. He drew in a swift breath when he saw the extensive maze of red laser beams crisscrossing the canyon floor. Taylor wouldn't have known to check. Hell, if he hadn't caught a brief glimpse on the frequency scan in his goggles display screen, he would have missed it.

"Hunter, can you bypass it?" Saber asked, staring at the red lines.

Hunter shook his head. "Dagger, what about you?" He asked.

Dagger raised an eyebrow. "You need to be talking to Jordan. She could do it. Me? I just kill things. She won't even let me near the vidcom to watch a movie. She says I killed the last one," he grunted.

"I might be able to," Trig replied, staring at the system. "There was one similar to this on a mission I did a couple of years ago. I need to see if we have the equipment to do it."

"Do it," Razor ordered. "What do you need?"

Trig snorted. "An electro-magnetic pulse controller."

Saber scowled at Trig. "Where in the *shewta* do you expect us to find one of those?"

"You're wearing it," Trig replied, looking at Saber's right leg.

..*

An hour later, Saber stood next to Trig as he synced the controller for his brace with the security system.

Trig explained that the signal that emitted the low pulses in the brace that enabled the contraction of the nerves and muscles in Saber's leg were essentially the same frequency as the security system.

"We need to stay as close to you as possible. The controller should keep the signal from being broken," Trig explained. "The key is that it will only sync with the surrounding signal for about one and a half meters. We need to stay within that diameter."

"Let's do this!" Saber growled, shifting uncomfortably.

"One thing I forgot to mention," Trig muttered as he gripped the rifle in his hand.

"What's that?" Saber snapped, glancing over his shoulder at Trig.

Trig grimaced. "It is going to drain the battery life on your brace," he muttered with an apologetic look. "You're going to be using a lot more energy."

"What about his leg?" Hunter asked with a frown.

Trig glanced down at Saber's leg before looking up again. "It might get a little twitchy, too," he added.

Saber could already have told Trig that. At the moment, his right leg was tingling and felt like he had a line of those damn insects the humans called ants climbing up it. He had made the mistake of stepping in a bed of them when he was back on Earth. It was an experience he wasn't likely to ever forget. Dagger and Hunter had laughed their asses off when he stripped out of his clothes and ended up in a pool of water, at least until they joined him.

"Can we just do this?" Saber asked through clenched teeth. "It feels like those insects from Earth are in my pants again."

"Goddess!" Dagger hissed with a shudder. "That was a miserable experience."

"Yes," Saber agreed. "Now, I'm heading out to find Taylor. If you are going, get in a circle."

Chapter 23

"She and the boy were here," Dagger said, glancing at the skid in the back of the cave.

"I know they were here," Saber said in aggravation. "What I want to know is why she and the boy are not still here or why she left the skid."

Ace glanced over. "The skid still has power, so that wasn't the reason," he added.

Hunter knelt near the entrance. "She wasn't alone," he said, rising up and looking at the other prints. "There were at least three others here."

Saber walked over to where Hunter was standing. He glanced down, following the same tracks as Hunter. He knelt beside Hunter, wincing when his leg protested. His fingers traced one footprint.

"It belongs to a female," he said. "Look at the size and stride."

He rose, grimacing when he staggered slightly. He shook his head when Hunter reached out to him. Glancing around, he saw the remains of a small fire and the tarp he had given her to keep warm.

"I don't think she left on her own. She wouldn't have left this," Razor said, holding up Taylor's notebook.

Saber walked over to Razor and held his hand out for the notebook. His fingers wrapped around the strange writing pad with Taylor's doodles all over it. She had several of them and she liked to carry at least one with her at all times. He remembered giving her a set for her birthday. He had begged Jag pick some up from her world and ship them to him.

He caressed the cover before opening it to where the pen was stuck. Over the last five years, he had learned to read Taylor's language. It had helped to pass the time and he found the flow of language unusual. He frowned as he read what she had written. A soft chuckle escaped him. She hadn't been lying when she said she had been making a list of things he would have to do to get back in her good graces.

"What is it?" Dagger asked, peering over his shoulder with a frown.

Saber grinned. "She likes being on top," he replied without thinking.

Dagger chuckled. "So does Jordan," he retorted in amusement. "It leaves my hands free."

Saber's grin turned to a scowl when Hunter ripped the notebook out of his hands and scanned the page. He tried to snatch it back, but Hunter jerked it away. A snarl escaped him when Hunter continued reading it.

"That's private," Saber snapped, finally retrieving the notebook.

Hunter's gaze locked on Saber's face. "You will either claim her as your *Amate* or I will forbid you from seeing her again," he growled.

"Forbid me! I have already claimed her as mine," Saber ground out, stepping closer to Hunter and glaring at him.

"It is not official until she wears your mark," Hunter replied in a hard voice. "She is still under my protection until then."

The fingers on Saber's left hand tightened around the writing pad as he resisted the urge to plant it in the middle of Hunter's face. Instead, he leaned his rifle against his leg so he could pull his shirt open far enough to slide the notebook inside. Refastening his shirt, he reached for his rifle once again before glaring at Trig.

"We need to track where they were taken," he snapped.

Trig nodded. "Fortunately, the sensors don't run more than a few meters inside the canyon. We can spread out. The fresh sand will work in our favor."

"I don't think so," Ace murmured, nodding toward the entrance.

An expletive escaped Saber when he turned and saw the dark shapes of several figures standing just outside the opening, their weapons trained on the entrance to the cave. Shouldering his weapon, he watched as a figure stepped into the entrance. He couldn't see the face of the person, but the figure was clearly that of a woman.

Her hands rose and she slowly removed her helmet to stare at each of the men. She raised her eyebrow at the weapons aimed at her. Her gaze moved from one to the other before she finally spoke.

"Which one of you is called Saber?" She asked.

A frown creased Saber's brow. "I am. Who are you?" He asked, not lowering his weapon.

The female's gaze locked on his face. "I am Maridi. Where is the other Trivator?" She asked with a frown. "PT Taylor said there were seven of you."

Saber lowered his weapon and took a step forward. "Dead," he replied. "He was killed by a Drethulan several kilometers from here."

The woman's mouth tightened and she nodded. "They are nasty creatures. I hope you eliminated all of them," she hissed.

"We did," Hunter replied.

Maridi nodded. "Very good. Follow me," she ordered, replacing her helmet and turning on her heel.

"Where?" Saber demanded, glancing out the door at the others with Maridi.

Maridi glanced over her shoulder. A wave of frustration swept through him that he couldn't see her eyes. His hand tightened on his weapon as he waited.

"To where PT Taylor is," Maridi replied before walking out.

Saber glanced at Dagger and Trig as they stepped closer, their weapons still at the ready. He saw the wary expression on their faces. This entire mission had been rather unorthodox.

"How the hell did they know we were here?" Trig asked. "I know we didn't break the beam."

"I don't know, but I plan to find out," Saber muttered, turning his gaze back to Razor and Hunter. "What do you think?" He asked.

"I think we are about to find out what is really going on," Razor said with a grim expression.

Saber nodded and drew in a deep breath before he stepped out into the bright sunlight where Maridi was waiting. Unease filled him as more guards filed in behind them. He had to hand it to Taylor. If there was trouble to be found, she would not only find it, she would jump into it feet first.

I think I will be using those ties she wanted on ***her****,* Saber thought as he broke into an uneven jog.

..*

A short time later, Saber stared up at the massive entrance at the end of the canyon. He glanced back and noted that it was well hidden by the winding passage and rock formations of the canyon. Turning back around, he climbed the staircase that was cut into the stone.

He was surprised that their escorts had not confiscated their weapons. A grimace crossed his face when his right leg protested the movement of climbing the stair. So much for taking it easy like the healer instructed him, he thought.

Maridi paused at the entrance and waved her hand. Saber suspected that there was some type of defense system in place because she didn't move for several seconds. He glanced over his shoulder when Dagger leaned forward.

"Something tells me we don't want to just run through the door," Dagger reflected dryly. "Either the Western region has technology that we weren't aware of, or they have help from another species."

"I doubt it is the Waxians or Drethulans," Saber replied before he stepped forward when Maridi turned to look down at them.

"The Kassisans," Dagger muttered before he followed.

Saber glanced around the entrance. Maridi removed her helmet and tucked it under her arm before she turned to address them. He didn't complain. It gave his eyes time to adjust to the dark interior.

"Do not try to leave the complex without either myself or one of my guards. We are the only ones who know how to work the security system. Before you think to try to force one of us to reveal how it works, I can assure you we will die first. There is more to this fight than our lives. You will understand that shortly. I would like to welcome you to the Dises V rebel base," Maridi said in a calm voice before she turned and waved her hand again.

Saber drew in a deep breath when the wall in front of them parted and a massive hanger appeared with a long line of fighters. He heard Hunter's low curse. Something told him that there would be hell to pay when he got Razor alone.

"Follow me," Maridi said, turning and walking down the long, narrow bridge that led to the hanger.

Saber glanced at Razor when he walked up beside him. "Did you forget to tell us something?" He asked dryly.

"There is concern that the council might be compromised," Razor replied bluntly. "The information was on a Need to Know basis."

"Did you know about this?" Hunter asked, waving his hand at the fighters.

Razor's mouth tightened. "No," he admitted. "I knew about the base located in the mountains."

Maridi glanced over her shoulder. "This one just came online in the past month," she stated. "It was important to keep it as secret as possible."

Razor's eyes narrowed on several unknown warriors walking toward them. The one man and one woman had light blue skin and piercing silver eyes. His lips tightened when they returned his gaze with a cold assessing one.

"Who are they?" He asked Maridi.

"Elpidiosians. They are allies of the Kassisans… now," she chuckled. "They are known for their fighting ability and technology."

"I believe I will be having a meeting with the Kassisan ambassador when I return to Rathon," Razor retorted.

"I have not met him, but my father has," Maridi replied. "He said Lord Ajaska Ja Kel Coradon is a very astute male."

"Judicious enough to withhold information that should have been shared," Razor said with a bite in his voice.

"Saber!"

Saber turned when he heard Taylor's joyous cry. He handed his rifle to Hunter and opened his arms. A moment later, he had Taylor wrapped around him.

He ignored the soft chuckles around him and pulled back far enough to look down into her face to make sure that she was alright. Seeing her shining eyes and happy grin, he bent and captured her lips in a passionate kiss. He reluctantly pulled back when he felt a tap on his shoulder.

"I might remind you where we are," Hunter informed him in exasperation. "Hello, Taylor."

"Hi Hunter," Taylor grinned. "I'm glad you aren't dead."

Hunter chuckled. "I am, as well, Taylor," he replied dryly.

Saber released Taylor's legs so that she could slide down his length and back to the floor. He took his rifle back from Hunter and wrapped his arm around Taylor's small waist. He could feel her looking around with a frown.

"Where's Cain?" She asked.

Saber's arm tightened around her waist when Dagger explained that he didn't make it. He could feel the tremble that swept through her slender body. He suddenly remembered her notepad that he had tucked in his shirt. He started to reach for it, then paused when he heard Razor talking.

"The patrol that was following us was mostly made up of Waxians," Razor explained when Maridi turned to look at them with concern.

"Mostly," Trig grunted in distaste. "There were three Drethulans with them."

"We thought that we had killed them, but the bastards don't die very easily," Ace added. "One came up behind Cain and struck him."

"Oh, poor Cain," Taylor whispered, shaking her head.

"They were more conditioned to survive the sand storm than the Waxians," Dagger said. "I didn't realize they could burrow under the sand the way they did."

"Neither did I," Saber admitted.

"Which is why each of the bases that have been set up are located in rock," a male voice pointed out.

"Father," Maridi greeted, bowing to him.

"Father!" Lonnie cried out, running to his father.

"Londius," the man said, bending down to pick up the boy and holding him before he looked at the odd group of warriors in front of him. "Thank you for saving my son. Maridi will show you where you can get cleaned up and eat. Once you have refreshed yourselves, I will meet with you."

"We left the transport at the entrance to the canyon," Saber suddenly said in concern. "It might be seen by one of the numerous patrols."

"It has been taken care of, along with all tracks," the male assured him. "I will meet with you soon."

"I told Maridi that you would be staying with me," Taylor whispered, staring up at him. "I won't take no for an answer."

Saber chuckled and hugged her to him. "Have you ever?" He teased as they began following Maridi through the hidden base.

Chapter 24

Saber followed Taylor when she veered off from the others. They walked down several corridors. Each one section was either still under construction or in use. He was impressed with the little that he saw. There were several species he was not familiar with and he paused to study them. One male turned to look at him when the person he was listening to stopped talking. A shiver of warning ran through Saber when he saw the icy blue in the male's eyes swirl with color. He hoped to the Gods that Razor and the council knew what they were doing.

"Where are we going?" Saber asked, frowning and turning in a circle when he saw several people from the Western region talking with a group from the East.

Taylor glanced over her shoulder and smiled. "I was given a room in the lower section. Maridi said most of you would be in the upper level. It is still under construction in places, but that was the only other quarters available at the moment since the arrival of the new crew," she explained.

"What new crew?" Saber asked with a sense of growing worry. "What is going on?"

Taylor paused and looked at Saber before shaking her head and pressing a kiss to his lips. The look in her eyes promised she would share what she knew the moment they were alone. He nodded, gripping her hand in one of his while his other hand held his laser rifle.

"This place is huge," Taylor said with a slight smile as she stepped into a lift. "Hang on, these things move pretty fast."

Saber wrapped his arm around her and stumbled slightly when the lift began to drop. Taylor held on to the bar behind him. She wasn't kidding. It felt like his stomach was in his throat by the time the damn thing stopped.

"*That*… is dangerous," Saber grumbled as the doors opened.

Taylor grinned up at him. "Lonnie and I rode it like a dozen times before Commander Atlas caught us," she admitted, grabbing his hand and pulling him down the empty corridor.

"Commander Atlas?" Saber asked.

Taylor nodded, stopping in front of a door and swiping the door with her palm. "Lonnie and Maridi's father. He is in charge of the Dises V rebellion. He told me that you were okay," she added before stepping inside the room.

"How did he know?" Saber demanded, following her into the room. "What is going on, Taylor?"

Taylor turned the moment the door closed behind him and wrapped her arms around his neck. He leaned his rifle next to the door and wound his arms around her, pulling her close. For a moment, he didn't care about anything but the fact that she was safe.

Taylor released a deep sigh before leaning back to look up at him. "Razor was right," she whispered.

"The Drethulans are preparing for war and they aren't the only ones."

"How...," Saber started to say before his words were silenced by Taylor's lips.

A groan escaped him when she threaded her fingers through his hair. A small tremor shook her body. It took a moment for him to realize that it was a soft giggle. He reluctantly pulled back and raised an eyebrow at her.

"I don't want to talk about what the future might hold right now. I want to talk about the present. You have sand in your hair," she whispered.

A soft chuckle escaped Saber. "That tends to happen when you are buried in a sandstorm," he said.

"Come on. I know how to fix that," she replied with a grin.

"I bet you do," Saber muttered, reaching for the fastening on his shirt. "Oh, I found this, as well."

Taylor's eyes widened when she saw him pull her writing pad out of his shirt. A rosy blush rose up her neck and into her cheeks when she saw him open it to the list she was making. Biting her lip, she tilted her head and gave him a mischievous grin.

"I take it you read it," she murmured, reaching up to play with the end of her braid.

"I want you to show me how much you like being on top," he ordered in a husky voice.

Taylor's face lit up. "I thought you'd never ask," she teased.

Saber's eyes remained glued to Taylor as they both stripped out of their clothes. He started to reach down and remove the brace on his right leg, but stopped when Taylor ran her fingers across his flat stomach. He saw her gaze was on the brace.

"They gave it to you," she whispered.

"Yes," he replied in a husky voice.

She swallowed. "It's still in prototype mode," she continued, sliding her hand down over the fabric. "I got the idea from the technology they were using to help Hunter."

"That's what they said," Saber admitted, gritting his teeth. "Ah, Taylor..."

Taylor's eyes jerked up to meet his. "Does it hurt?" She asked with a worried frown.

Saber gave her a crooked grin. "It doesn't, but I do," he said. "All I can think about is you on top."

"Oh… OH!" She mouthed before blushing again. "Right, shower first."

Saber looked up at the ceiling and breathed a sigh of relief; for the first time in years, he felt… normal. Yes, they were in a strange base. Yes, their lives were still in danger.

But, he reasoned, *when hasn't the universe been a slightly crazy place to live in?*

He looked down when he felt the cool air of the room against his leg. A shiver ran through him when Taylor ran her fingers over the long scar on his leg before she tossed the brace onto a nearby chair.

"Shower?" he asked tightly when she trailed her fingers up his leg to his hip.

"This way," she whispered.

Saber's gaze swept down over Taylor's curvy figure. Deciding he had been restrained enough, he released a soft growl and started after her. Taylor shrieked and giggled as she hurried into the room.

He watched as she stepped into the shower unit and turned. His hand tightened on the door frame and watched her as the unit came on. Water fell like rain from the top of the unit, catching on her eyelashes and running in small droplets down over her shoulders to her breasts.

"You are so beautiful," he whispered, gazing at her.

"So are you," she said, lifting her hand to him. "Catch me, Saber. Catch me and never let me go again."

Saber heard the pain in her voice and knew at that moment just how deeply he had hurt her. He reached for her hand, gripping it tightly in his as he stepped under the soft flow.

His lips captured hers in a desperate kiss. This time, she opened for him. A soft moan escaped him when she responded to his passion. He loved the way Taylor kissed. It was not something the males and females of his species did. The Trivator's form of kissing involved leaving a scent mark on their mate; but this, this was something far more tantalizing than leaving his scent against her skin.

He broke the kiss to run his lips along her jaw down to her neck. He felt her body tremble and she tilted her head to give him free access to her. Her hands ran over his shoulders.

"I'm going to put my mark right there," he whispered against her throat. "When we return to Rathon, I ask that you accept my mark as your *Amate*, as I will wear yours if you accept my claim."

"You bet your ass I do," Taylor replied, turning her head, her lips just a breath away from his.

Saber's laugh filled the shower unit as he picked her up and pressed her against the wall. Taylor kissed him deeply before she rested her forehead against his and gazed into his eyes. She brushed her hands through his hair before cupping his cheeks.

"I love you, Saber," she murmured.

Saber brushed a kiss against her lips. "I love you more, Taylor Sampson. You are a gift from the Goddess," he said.

"From the stars," she replied, closing her eyes as he slid his hand over ass. "I want to wash you."

Saber groaned and buried his face against her neck for a moment. He swore she was going to kill him. The idea of her hands touching him, running all over him, stroking…

"Okay," he said, using the term he had frequently heard on Earth.

He gripped Taylor's waist and slid her down his slick body. Stepping back, he swallowed and gritted his teeth when Taylor flashed him an innocent smile. His eyes followed her as she poured some of the cleanser into her hand and rubbed her hands together.

Something tells me that payback is about to start, he thought vaguely just before she motioned for him to bend over so she could wash his hair.

A soft moan escaped when he felt the way she was running her fingers across his scalp. He tilted his head back when she moved her hands down over his shoulders. It was as if she was making love to every inch of his body with her touch.

His gaze followed her slender fingers as she ran the soapy solution over his skin. She paused and traced a light scar that he hadn't bothered having removed. Her hand moved down to his and she leaned in to briefly kiss the mark she had traced before she lifted his hand and ran her hand over his palm.

Soft skin against rough, just like Taylor and I, he thought as a sensual haze clouded his mind.

Her fingers tangled with his for a moment before she trailed her fingers up the back of his hand and around to the sensitive flesh of his inner wrist. His breath caught as she stepped closer to him and ran her hand along the underside of his arm.

"I love touching you," she whispered as she caressed his chest. He had a light coating of hair across it. There was just enough that she could tangle her fingers in it. She had seen Hunter and Dagger. Both of them were devoid of hair on their chests. "For the last five years, I've touched you, but not in the way I wanted to. Not until…."

Saber silenced her with his lips. He kissed her with a gentleness that brought tears to her eyes. He brushed them away with his lips before running his nose along her cheek up to the corner of her eye. With each stroke, he made sure that she could feel the love he had for her.

"I was wrong," he whispered. "You are such an incredible woman, Taylor. You capture the light and brighten the world with it. I was in a dark place, afraid to see that light vanish when you realized that I was not the warrior that I had been."

"But, you are," she said, looking up at him with a tender smile. "You are my warrior. You caught me, Saber, and captured my heart that first day in the cafeteria."

"Goddess, Taylor, I don't deserve you, but I swear I will never let you go," Saber said in a voice hoarse with emotion.

Taylor didn't say anything; she showed him. Palming more soap, she ran her hands over his other arm and down his chest, reaching lower. Saber's shuddering breath echoed throughout the bathroom when she wrapped her hands around his throbbing cock. His hands shot out and he plastered them against the walls of the shower.

His eyelids drooped as he watched her caress him. His fingers curled when her hand slipped down to cup his heavy sack. He would give her time now, but by the Goddess, his turn would come next. He would take her with a passion that would leave her in no doubt that he was claiming her.

"Ahhhh," Saber moaned, his head falling back as she continued to stroke him.

A soft chuckle mixed with his agonized cry. Taylor was well aware of what she was doing to him. If she were trying to torture him, she was doing an excellent job of it.

He knew he could last no longer when she started working her way back up him. Bending, he helped her stand, holding her away from his over-sensitive flesh. With a trembling hand, he brushed her wet hair back from her face.

"Touch me no more, Taylor. I have little control left and I swear that your pleasure will come before my own this night," he warned her in a rough voice. "Wait… Wait for me in our bed."

"Saber," she whispered.

"I want you, Taylor," he whispered. "Give me this, please. I have been selfish long enough."

"I want another all-nighter when we get out of here," she said. "For now, I'll take an all-afternoon."

"Goddess, you don't fight fair," he accused hoarsely when she stepped out of the shower.

"Just wait until you get in the bed," she retorted with a sultry gaze that ran up and down his body. "Don't make me wait, Saber."

***

Saber closed his eyes and drew in a dozen deep, calming breaths. He looked up and caught his reflection in the mirror. Straightening up, he quickly finished washing and rinsed off. He grabbed one of the towels lying next to the sink.

He quickly dried his body, pausing briefly on his right leg. It was a little stiff and sore, but it felt stronger than it had since he woke after the mission. He stepped out of the bathroom. The towel in his hand paused as he dried his hair.

His gaze froze on Taylor lying on their bed. She was watching him with a small smile on her lips. The dim lighting along the upper wall cast a soft glow around her. She had dried her hair as best she could with the towel and combed it out. A length of golden brown hung over her shoulder, barely covering her breast. Her left breast was bare.

His hand fell to his side as he slowly walked across the room. Tossing the towel on the end of the bed, he sank down beside her. He reached out, touching the end of her hair.

"So beautiful," he whispered, sliding his hand up under her hair and along her breast. "And, so perfect for me."

He turned his face into her hand when she raised it to run her fingers along his jaw. Pressing a kiss to the center, he raised his other hand and pulled her toward him. Their lips met in the middle, opening and inhaling each other's breath as if they were one.

His hand slid down her throat to her shoulder before moving down far enough for him to cup her breast. Pressing small kisses to the corner of her mouth, he continued along her jaw. A wave of warmth swept through him when Taylor arched toward him, offering him full access to her body.

He opened his mouth and scraped his sharp teeth along the distended nipple before he sucked on it. Her gasp and the scent of her arousal washed over him. A rumble of pleasure escaped him and his other hand moved down to slide between her legs. He could feel the slickness of her arousal coating the soft light brown curls that protected her womanhood.

"My *Amate*," he whispered against her breast before he pulled away.

Turning, he knelt over her. His eyes glowed with his desire, turning them a deeper yellow-gold. His pupils were dilated and he was breathing in deep, slow, measured breaths as he gazed down at her.

"Saber," Taylor moaned, reaching up to touch his lips. "Love me."

"Forever, Taylor," he replied in a thick voice. "I am Saber. I belong to Taylor as she belongs to me. Forever will I tie my life to hers. I will care for, protect, and give my seed only to her. She is my *Amate*. You are my life, Taylor."

Taylor swallowed. "I am Taylor. I belong to Saber as he belongs to me. I give to him my love forever. Forever will I tie my life to his. I will care for, protect, and cherish him as he cherishes me. You are my *Amate*. I love you," she whispered tearfully, rubbing her thumb along the corner of his mouth. "I love you so much, Saber, for so very, very long."

"Not long enough," Saber assured her. "It will never be long enough."

He lowered himself down over her, running his lips over her breasts and down over her stomach. Each kiss, each touch, burned into his soul. His whole body was alive with feeling. Her moans and heated cries filled the air. It was music to his ears. Her pleas for more fired his blood. His hands slid under the curve of her buttocks and he lifted her so he could drink from her. His tongue played with the swollen nub when he parted her to his touch. He was rewarded when her body stiffened and a smothered scream escaped her.

He slid his hand upward, driving his fingers into her as she came. He could feel the walls of her vagina pulse with her release. Knowing he could not last long this first time, he wanted to draw out her pleasure. Now was the time to mark her as his.

His fingers slid from her slick warmth. His gaze locked on her as he pulled her legs up around his waist. He leaned forward, aligning his cock with her silky entrance. Her eyes opened and she looked at him with a dazed expression.

"Forever, Taylor," he muttered as he slowly impaled her.

"Saber!" Taylor cried out, arching into him and holding on to his arms as he began to rock.

Saber clenched his teeth. He needed to wait until she was at the precipice. When she was, he would strike, marking her as his. The chemical in his mark would numb the pain and increase her pleasure as it bound her to him.

He increased his thrust, driving deeper each time until he felt they were truly one. Each thrust of his hips pulled his throbbing cock along her swollen channel. He could feel every silky inch of it as it sucked greedily for his seed.

Saber threw his head back and roared when Taylor's body stiffened around him, clamping down on him like a fist. His body trembled for a fraction of a second before he exploded inside her with a force that ripped a cry from his throat. Breathing heavily, he leaned forward and opened his mouth. Reciting his pledge to her, he bit down on the curve of her shoulder near her neck.

She writhed under him, her hands clawing at him for a brief moment before the heat of another orgasm locked her in its greedy grasp. Saber reluctantly released her neck and licked the wound. The puncture wounds would be healed by morning, but the mark of his teeth would never fade.

She is mine, Saber thought as a wave of calm settled over his soul.

Chapter 25

Saber ran his fingers down along Taylor's flushed cheek. His eyebrow rose when she snorted in her sleep and rolled onto her side, hugging his pillow. He closed his eyes when she wiggled back against him and tucked the curve of her ass against him.

"You are a very, very dangerous woman, my *Amate,*" Saber whispered, leaning forward to press a kiss against her bare shoulder. "I am the luckiest warrior in the world to have you by my side."

Taylor mumbled in her sleep. It sounded suspiciously like 'you bet your ass, old man'. Shaking his head, he pressed another kiss to her shoulder before releasing a sigh when he heard a chime at the outer door. Rising from the bed, he grabbed the towel and wrapped it around his waist before stepping over to the door and pressing his palm against the panel.

"What?" He asked in aggravation.

Hunter glanced up and down before his gaze moved to the dim room behind him. "I'm warning you now, Saber, you better not break Taylor's heart again. If I don't kill you first, you'll wish I had after Jesse and Jordan get a hold of you," he bit out in a quiet, menacing voice. "Get dressed. We have a meeting with Commander Atlas and Razor."

Saber nodded and started to pull away. "She wears my mark on her," Saber replied quietly. "Once we are back on Rathon, we will complete the ceremony. I will not turn her away again, Hunter. I understand the gift I have been given."

"It's about time," Hunter muttered.

Saber palmed the door shut, but not before he caught Hunter's muttered statement. A soft chuckle escaped him. Yes, it was about time. He glanced at where Taylor was peacefully sleeping. Drawing in a deep breath, he shook his head in exasperation. He didn't want to leave her for fear that she would disappear.

"No one ever told me just how hard it was to have an *Amate,*" he muttered.

He quickly pulled on the set of clean clothes that Taylor had picked up when she heard that Maridi had gone to retrieve him and the others. He didn't bother with his leg brace. The power was depleted on it. While it would still give him support, he figured he would not need it until later.

By then, he hoped he could find a way to recharge it. His gaze swept back to Taylor. She had rolled onto her back. Her right arm was now thrown up over her head in relaxed abandon. If anyone knew how to recharge it, Taylor would, he thought with a sense of pride. Refocusing on the task at hand, he turned toward the door once again.

Two minutes later, he was striding back to the lift from hell with Hunter. He turned and faced the front. A grin curved his lips when he saw Hunter grip the hand bar.

"Taylor loves this thing," Saber shared with a sigh.

Hunter chuckled. "I can understand why. Do you remember when she learned how to ride the air bike?" He reminded Saber.

Saber's face twisted at the memory. "She scared the hell out of me," he murmured. "I love her, Hunter. I've known that since I first saw her, but I never realized how much until she walked out of the door the night after…." He paused and drew in a deep breath as the lift started to slow. "When I found out she had been captured, it was like someone had ripped out my heart."

"I know what you were going through, Saber. It was not always easy for Jesse and I," Hunter responded with a weary sigh.

Saber nodded to the other men as they entered what looked like the main control room. In the center was a huge holovid with troop movements. He noticed Hunter's mouth tightening as he stared at the classified information. It was obvious that Razor hadn't shared everything about the mission.

"What is going on, Razor?" Saber asked, looking around the command center. "This wasn't built in the last six months. A command center this large must have been under construction for a number of years."

"True," Hunter growled with a glare at his older brother.

Razor sighed and nodded. He glanced at Commander Atlas. The commander gave him a sharp nod to continue.

"As you know, a new star system joined the Alliance a few years ago. There was concern voiced by many within the Alliance council of their acceptance due to their technological advancements," Razor began.

"I hate to tell you this, Razor, but the Trivators are not without our own advances," Trig interjected dryly.

Razor shot Trig a heated look. "I'm well aware of our advancements, Trig. The Kassisans and the Elpidiosians are slightly ahead of us in certain areas. Still, some of our more recent advances in weaponry, including the signal disrupter we are using, are because of their willingness to share. Before joining the Alliance, the former ruler of Kassis and their present ambassador, Ajaska Ja Kel Coradon, was suspicious of increased hostile activities that were taking place within the star systems, both under the Kassisan protection and ones that were considered off limits due to their lack of intergalactic space travel. Those hostilities have increased since their incorporation into the Alliance Council."

"Define hostile," Dagger demanded, leaning against a table near the center map.

"They tried to assassinate my sons and myself," a deep voice said dryly. "I consider that hostile."

"Lord Ja Kel Coradon," Commander Atlas greeted.

"Greetings, Commander… High Chancellor," Ajaska said with a slight bow of his head.

Saber stared at the Kassisan ambassador with a growing sense of concern. This wasn't a typical diplomatic meeting on a planet torn apart by civil unrest any more than this was a typical rebel base.

There was more going on than he or the other warriors had been told.

"Can someone please tell me what in the *shewta* is going on?" Ace finally asked from behind the group.

..*

Ajaska glanced at Commander Atlas and nodded his head. The commander pursed his lips before he barked out a sharp order for the room to be cleared and sealed. Within minutes, the only ones left in the room were the Kassisan, Commander Atlas, and the Trivators.

"How well do you trust the men in this room, Razor?" Ajaska asked in a quiet voice.

"With my life," Razor replied immediately.

Ajaska chuckled. "Something tells me that is not something you would normally say," he responded with an assessing look.

"It's not," Razor answered in a clipped tone.

Ajaska released a sigh and walked over to the map. He stood studying it for several long minutes before he turned. His face was cut into a hard mask, highlighting the long scar along one side of it.

"I won't tell you everything, so don't bother asking," he began, looking around the group with a serious expression. "What I am going to tell you might not make sense, or even be believable, but I can assure you it is all real. Shortly after we joined the Alliance, one of our shuttles was returning from a diplomatic mission. It was overtaken by a Tearant warship…"

Saber listened as Ajaska Ja Kel Coradon outlined the initial threat against the Houses of Kassis and the unexpected alliance with Elpidios that led to the discovery of a special ship… a ship that went places and a special warrior who saw things that warned of events to come.

"If you are worried about influencing the future, why are you telling us?" Trig asked. "Why didn't this 'warrior' of yours tell you how to prevent it?"

Ajaska turned a steely gaze to Trig. "Because he understands more than anyone that such knowledge could work both ways. He was only able to obtain a limited amount of data during his mission. What information he did record made it essential that we prepare as much as possible. War is coming, the only uncertainty is the outcome."

"If it is just the Drethulans, we can strike now," Ace argued, standing up and glaring at Ajaska. "Why go to such extremes by building a base here? Why not just eliminate them?"

Ajaska's lips tightened. "There are more than the Drethulans. There is another group, one that has been building up forces for centuries."

"Who?" Hunter asked.

"Ones that we faced in a previous life," Ajaska replied quietly. "That is all I can tell you at the moment. We are still trying to interpret what we do know. Our single most important advantage is the knowledge we have that it is going to happen. We are currently taking steps to infiltrate the enemy as much as we can in an effort to minimize the devastation."

"The Kassisan at the fortress," Saber murmured.

Ajaska grimaced and nodded. "He is just one of many. I have kept a low profile among the Alliance Council in an effort to keep much of what we know a secret. It was also essential to give the impression that the Kassisans are not interested in the issues going on in this star system."

"Why are you?" Dagger asked with a raised eyebrow. He waved his hand around the control room. "I see at least a dozen technological advances that we are just working on. The power source for this base alone would take up half a mountain, yet unless you were able to build it underground without anyone ever seeing a damn thing, then I would have to say you are ahead of us in energy technology."

A slight smile curved Ajaska's lips. "We have a common interest, Trivator," he assured Dagger in a quiet voice. "The safety of the star systems is paramount to the welfare of us all. The fall of one can easily lead to the fall of the entire Alliance. I don't particularly relish seeing my planet enslaved, or worse."

A low murmur swept around the group. Saber glanced at the Kassisan before turning to look at Razor and Hunter. His hand ran down to his leg. This mission showed that he was still capable of fighting. He would do whatever was necessary to protect Taylor and his people.

"Why here?" He asked, looking at the Kassisan. "Why Dises V?"

Ajaska turned to look at Saber. "Dises V is where the Drethulans obtain the ore necessary to build up their forces. We must prevent that. The production has just started, but if it continues, it will not only give the Drethulans and their Allies the resources they need to fight, it will also cause massive environmental destruction. Dises V will be the first planet to fall, Trivator. We must make sure that does not happen."

"The Waxian forces have taken over the Western Region. Their annihilation of the Western Council was foretold by Ajaska's warrior. The Western council refused to acknowledge the threat by the Waxians, despite the warnings given to them. This refusal is what led to their assassination when they began to realize that the warnings given to them were valid," Commander Atlas said, stepping up.

"Then, how was this base built?" Hunter asked with a frown. "As Dagger said, this structure would take years to build. I cannot see the military being unaware of it."

"It wasn't," Commander Atlas stated. "I was the military for the Western Region. Ajaska approached me with evidence five years ago. Construction began without the Council's knowledge a few months later."

"What about the Eastern Region? Why enslave the people from that region?" Saber asked.

"We don't," Commander Atlas replied. "The Eastern Council is just as corrupt as our own. The Waxian and Drethulans have purchased the council. They are using the propaganda that the West is behind the recent enslavement of their people to create unrest and explain for the massive disappearance of their people. When I proposed a military attack on those running the mines, I was labeled a traitor. I, and several other senior military officers, disappeared before we could be arrested and sent to the mines."

"The rebel base in the mountains of the Crescent Moon," Saber murmured.

"Yes," Commander Atlas replied. "It is run by my Eastern counterpart, Commander Faila. Fortunately, most of the construction of this base has been completed. What is left can be done without drawing the attention to the current ruling forces, especially now that both the East and the West are under the control of the Drethulans and the Waxians."

"Our forces…," Hunter started to say in concern, looking at Razor.

Razor shook his head. "I contacted the Alliance Council earlier," he replied grimly. "They have ordered the Trivator forces to leave. They believe that individual strife on a planet should be handled by the planet's ruling governments. The ambassador to Dises V insists this is an internal matter. They have specified that all Trivator military support here to protect the medical aid is no longer necessary. The Council has agreed. All Trivator military troops have withdrawn."

"Except us," Dagger muttered, looking around the room. "So, where does that leave us?"

Razor turned his gaze to the small group of men. "Behind enemy lines," he replied grimly.

Chapter 26

Saber gazed around him with a new appreciation. Ajaska Ja Kel Coradon's fantastical story that began in the past and moved to the future before returning to the present was difficult to wrap his mind around. The Kassisan refused to give any other details about the supposed 'ship' or the warrior who piloted it. All he would say was that some things were best left unexplained.

Saber wasn't sure if he agreed with the Kassisan, but deep down, he knew the male was speaking the truth. There were just too many facts that he knew, and was able to prove when he shared recent Intel that Razor and Hunter were able to confirm as being accurate.

"What do you think?" Dagger asked, matching his stride.

"That we'd better be prepared," Saber finally said. "The combined forces of the Waxian and Drethulan forces do not concern me. Our military is four times the size of theirs and we are better trained. Neither one of those species has ever had a military force under one rule because they are too busy either killing each other or looking for credits."

"Until now," Dagger pointed out, folding his arms across his chest. "The fact that they are both working together here on Dises V shows something is not right."

"Until now," Saber agreed, looking at Dagger when he suddenly touched his arm. "What's wrong?" He asked when he saw the serious look in Dagger's eyes.

"I think I know the warrior that Ajaska was talking about," Dagger reluctantly admitted. He glanced around, running a hand through his hair. "I don't know why I didn't piece it together at first."

"What happened?" Saber asked.

"It was after Jordan and I escaped from the Spaceport," Dagger muttered, his eyes dark with memories. "The starship we were in was damaged. I had to make an emergency landing on a moon that was filled with Gartaians of all things. While we were there, a strange red crystal ship appeared out of nowhere."

Saber released a low curse. "Did you tell Hunter or Razor about this?" He asked in disbelief.

Dagger shook his head, staring blankly down the hallway as if he was still locked in his memories. "No, I wasn't in a 'good place', as Jordan would call it, for almost a year, if you remember," he replied with a bitter twist of his lips.

"Yes, I remember," Saber murmured. "What happened?"

Dagger's lips twitched. "I met some of the strangest creatures I have ever seen in my life," he chuckled with a shake of his head. "Two bumbling Frenchmen from Earth who drank too much, two service bots that I wouldn't wish on my worst enemy, and a man who was more machine than living tissue."

Saber stared at Dagger with a raised eyebrow, waiting for him to continue. A snarl escaped him when his friend didn't say anything. Dagger jerked, as if he was lost in that time instead of standing next to Saber.

"Well?" Saber finally asked.

Dagger shook his head. "His name was Jarmen," he replied in a quiet voice. "He was searching for someone, according to the two Frenchmen." Dagger looked back at Saber. "He helped me repair the starship, and he saved our lives when we were attacked. Then he, his unusual crew, and the red crystal ship just vanished," he finished quietly before he turned and started walking again.

..*

Saber didn't miss Dagger's use of phrases like 'appeared out of nowhere' and 'vanished'. He released a deep breath and paused in the hallway to look around. They were back in the landing bay.

It was three times the size of the landing bay aboard the typical Trivator warship. The hanger was filled with a wide variety of fighters, from old to new, from Dises V models to more advanced ones that he was not familiar with. His gaze scanned the workers. They were just as diverse as the fighters. He jerked in surprise when he saw a familiar figure sitting at one of the benches.

"Taylor," Saber muttered.

Dagger turned and glanced over to where Taylor was sitting at a workbench. Small flashes of light showed that she was working intently on something. She was a lot like her sister, Jordan, and yet different.

"I'll leave you for now. I think I'll go see if I can get any more information out of Hunter and let him know what I just told you. Trig and Ace have gone off exploring. They will report what they have found later this evening," Dagger said.

"I'll find out what Taylor knows as well," Saber muttered, not looking at Dagger.

Dagger's soft chuckle followed him as he strode across the hanger. He paused when a service bot crossed in front of him with a muttered apology before continuing. It was only when he was almost to the bench that he saw his leg brace.

"Taylor," Saber called in a soft voice.

Taylor's head jerked up and she glanced around. A chuckle escaped Saber when he saw that she was wearing a magnifying headset. Her beautiful brown eyes looked huge in the optical lenses. She blinked several times before she grinned up at him.

"Hey, you were gone again!" She said in a slightly accusing tone. "One of these days I'd like to wake up and have you still there beside me."

Saber could see the slight reserve that came into her eyes as she spoke. He knew what she was thinking, that he would reject her again like he had the last time. Reaching out, he gently removed the headset and set it down on the bench before bending and capturing her lips.

He felt her surprise before she relaxed into him and returned his kiss. She slowly rose off the stool she was sitting on and wound her arms around his neck. His hands slid down her back to her ass and he lifted her up so she could wrap her legs around his hips.

Several minutes later, they were both breathless as they stared at each other. Taylor tenderly ran her fingers down over his cheek before rubbing her thumb over his bottom lip. She smiled when he carefully lowered her back to the stool.

"What are you doing?" He asked, glancing down at the circular device she was working on.

Taylor released a sigh and turned back to the bench to pick up the watch-size controller. He reached for it when she handed it to him. Turning it over, he saw the steady glow.

"You recharged the controller," he murmured, turning it back over and studying it with a frown. "What is that?"

Taylor glanced at what he was pointing to. "An Elpidiosian red crystal," she said. "It took a few tries to understand how to tap into its energy without burning out the motherboard, but with the help of Commander Rue, I was able to do it. I don't think you'll have to worry about it going dead for at least a few centuries or more. The power inside just a tiny piece of these crystals is amazing!"

"Almost as amazing as you," Saber murmured, staring down at the glowing crystal that was no bigger than a granule of sand.

"I think you want some," Taylor replied with a happy sigh as she propped her chin up on the palm of her hand.

The clatter of a tool on the bench next to Taylor told Saber that the technician working at it was able to read the meaning of Taylor's statement by her tone and body language. The young male was trying not to get caught staring at Taylor. A low growl from Saber informed the male that he wasn't being successful.

"Have you eaten?" Saber asked, picking up the brace and the back casing to the controller.

Taylor shook her head. "No, I wanted to get this fixed first," she admitted, sliding off the stool.

"Let's go get something to eat," Saber muttered, shooting the young tech another look before he cupped Taylor's arm. "You are right," he muttered after they were several feet away.

"I was right about what?" Taylor asked, startled.

"I do want some," Saber replied with a grin.

Chapter 27

Later that evening, Taylor lay with her head tucked in the crook of Saber's shoulder. A soft sigh escaped her. She slid her fingers over his stomach and up his chest before laying her palm over his heart. Turning her head, she pressed a kiss against his heated flesh.

"What are we going to do next?" Taylor asked, rolling over onto her stomach so she could look down at him.

Saber turned his head and smiled tenderly at her worried expression. Lifting his hand, he brushed a long strand of her hair back behind her ear. He knew the answer to her question. Dagger and Trig had stopped by earlier when they were eating. Taylor had just left to go speak with Maridi and Lonnie.

"We leave in a few hours," he admitted. "There is not much we can do here without the Council's approval. Razor and Hunter need to return and hold a meeting."

"What happens if the Council refuses to listen to them?" Taylor asked with a frown. "They seem to be total knuckleheads."

Saber chuckled. "They are, at times," he agreed, leaning up to brush a kiss across the tip of her nose. "This time will be different. Ajaska will also address the Council. If the Alliance refuses to agree, Razor has the authority to overrule them as the High Chancellor. The Alliance needs the support of the Trivators;

without it, they are powerless to protect their star systems."

"Will he do it? Take control?" Taylor asked in surprise.

"Yes," he stated bluntly.

"Wow!" Taylor muttered, turning and curling up against him again. "Wow," she repeated after several long seconds of thinking of what that meant from everything she had learned in school.

"Yes, wow," he agreed, shifting so that he could roll until he was staring down at her. A wicked smile curved his lips. "I think I'd like to see if I can make you say that a few more times before we leave."

Taylor slid her hands down over his stomach again, this time heading in the opposite direction. He loved the challenging grin she gave him, as if daring him to try. His breath caught when she wrapped her hands around his cock and stroked him.

"Wow," she breathed when she felt him grow at her touch.

..*

"The cloaking device will keep us from being detected during departure until we meet with my starship," Ajaska explained as they walked around the exterior of the warship that he had arrived in.

"This is incredible," Trig muttered. "I could have used a device like that on more than half of my missions."

"You aren't the only one," Hunter agreed.

"Where's Razor?" Saber asked, looking around the hanger.

Hunter frowned. "Commander Atlas detained him as we were walking down here," he replied.

"There he is," Dagger observed. "It looks like Maridi found Sword and Thunder."

Saber turned and watched as Commander Atlas, Razor, Thunder, and Sword walked toward them. All three men had a grim expression on their faces. Both Sword and Thunder looked like they had seen better days. They weren't wearing the typical uniforms of a Trivator warrior, but the clothing of one of the nomads that inhabited the area.

"Sword, Thunder," he greeted.

"Hey, guys," Taylor said with a welcoming smile that didn't hide the worry in her eyes.

"We need to leave immediately," Razor said, glancing at Ajaska. "It would appear that one of your fears has come true."

Ajaska's face tightened. "Where?"

Saber frowned when Razor glanced at Taylor before he looked back at the others. He could tell from the muscle throbbing in Razor's jaw that he was beyond furious. Saber slid his arm around Taylor and pulled her protectively closer to him.

"Earth," Razor replied in a clipped tone.

Taylor's eyes widened. "Earth," she whispered. "But, it's under the protection of the Alliance. There are still Trivator forces there!"

"Not enough for what is coming, I'm afraid," Ajaska replied. "My ship is ready. I suggest we leave immediately."

"But, what about the people here?" Taylor asked, her gaze catching sight of Maridi and Lonnie further down the landing bay.

"We will be ready to strike," Commander Atlas assured her.

Saber watched as Commander Atlas signaled the hanger crew to prepare for a departure. The area darkened until only a series of red lights lit the area. It was enough for the workers to prepare for a night departure. Gripping Taylor's hand, he pulled her up the ramp behind him.

"Saber," Taylor whispered as they followed Ajaska and the others to the seats where they would strap in for takeoff. "Why would anyone attack Earth? Surely they know that the Trivator and Alliance have promised it protection. The humans are still rebuilding after… after you guys came."

"I know," Saber replied quietly. "The Alliance and the Trivator forces there will do everything they can to protect your world. We do not know what is happening yet. There will be a debriefing once we are on the Kassisan warship."

"I would like to be there," Taylor murmured.

Saber glanced at Hunter, who shook his head. He understood that even though Hunter understood Taylor's desire to attend the meeting, this was a matter of war. He glanced down and grimaced when he saw

Taylor shoot Hunter a murderous glare before she narrowed her eyes at him and smirked.

"Taylor," Saber growled under his breath.

Taylor sat back and folded her arms across her chest. "I didn't say anything," she muttered.

A silent groan swept through Saber. Taylor, Jordan, and Jesse would probably know more about what was going on than he did by the time everything was said and done. He gripped her hand as the small transport took off. It was going to be a long night.

..*

Later the next day, Taylor watched as Saber moved silently through their room on board Ajaska's warship. She waited, knowing that he had a lot on his mind. Her eyes followed his hands as he removed his shirt. A warm glow filled her as she ran her gaze over him.

"You really have bulked up," she murmured.

"What?" Saber asked, turning to look at her.

Taylor grinned. "I said you look yummy," she replied, wiggling her nose at him.

A startled chuckled escaped Saber and he strode over to the bed in their cabin. Taylor quickly rolled over onto her back when he braced his arms on each side of her, trapping her. He slid his knee onto the bed and pressed it against her hip.

"I do not believe I've ever heard a Trivator warrior called 'yummy' before," he murmured.

Taylor giggled and slid her hands up his chest. "Well, I could show you just how yummy you are," she suggested, walking her fingers back down and running them along the edge of his pants. "I could do a taste test. I'll start with your...."

Her giggle was smothered by his kiss. He had been gone all night and most of the day and she missed him. She had taken advantage of that time to contact both Jesse and Jordan to let them know that she and Saber were alright.

..*

Several hours earlier:

"When are you coming home?" Jordan had demanded, holding Helena, her and Dagger's daughter in her arms. "Here, go play with Leila," she finally whispered when Helena kept trying to squirm out of her arms.

Taylor laughed when she heard the two little girls squeal with delight. A moment later, Jesse's face appeared on the screen. She could feel Jesse searching her face to see if she was really happy.

"He loves me," Taylor said with a grin.

"Let me see your wrists," Jesse demanded.

Taylor shook her head, but raised both of her wrists. "We are having a ceremony when we get to Rathon. We are on a Kassisan warship at the moment and they don't have the equipment to do it here," she explained.

"He'd better or I'll kick his ass into next week," Jesse replied before she released a sigh. "I was so worried about you, Taylor."

"Me, too," Jordan admitted. "What happened?"

Taylor remembered wondering if she should tell her sisters everything that had happened. After a few seconds, she knew she should. They had never kept secrets from each other. Drawing in a deep breath, she told them everything – including why they were coming back in such a hurry.

"I can hack into the Council's system and see what they have," Jordan suggested.

"Jordan," Jesse admonished before she wiggled her nose. "I think you should break into Razor's instead. He would have more info than the Council."

Taylor laughed at Jordan's astonished gasp. "What about Kali? Shouldn't she know as well?" Jordan asked.

"I'll call her," Jesse promised. "If Earth is in trouble, she'll want to know. Her brother is still there."

"She'll kill Razor if he knew Destin was in trouble and didn't say anything or give her a warning," Taylor agreed.

"When will you be here?" Jesse asked, turning to look at Taylor.

"In less than a week," Taylor guessed. "The Kassisan warships are a little faster than the Trivator ones. At least this one is," she added.

"We'll be waiting," Jesse replied, reaching out to touch the screen. "I'm glad that you are safe. I miss you."

"I miss you both, too," Taylor murmured before she signed off. "I miss you, too," she repeated with a soft sigh.

..*

Saber pulled back to stare down at Taylor when he felt her withdrawal. He touched her cheek, brushing her hair back against the pillow. She gave him a sad smile.

"What is bothering you, little star?" Saber asked in a husky voice.

Taylor raised her hand again and touched his lips. "I was just thinking of my conversation with Jordan and Jesse earlier," she admitted.

A knowing look filled Saber's eyes and he slid down to lie beside her. Pulling her into his arms, he held her close. He felt the soft sigh that escaped her.

"Did you tell them what happened?" He asked, staring up at the ceiling.

"Uh-huh," she murmured, shaking her head.

"All of it?" He asked with a sigh of his own.

"Uh-huh," she whispered.

Saber drew in a deep breath. "Is Jordan going to hack into the Council's files to find out what is going on?" He asked in resignation.

"Nope," Taylor muttered. Saber felt his body relax before it stiffened at Taylor's next words. "She's going to hack into Razor's, and Jesse has invited Kali over so she knows what's going on too."

Saber closed his eyes and counted to one hundred before he opened them again. A reluctant smile curved his lips. This was the Sampson sisters at their best. Banding together, protecting, and not letting anything get in their way. Rolling, Saber braced himself on one elbow.

"What if I told you 'no', that I won't let you do it?" He asked with a twinkle in his eye.

Taylor grinned up at him as her fingers moved back down to the edge of his pants again. This time her fingers dipped inside, just enough to tease him. She looked at him with wide brown eyes gleaming with mischief.

"How do you feel about trolls in the house?" She asked.

To be continued: **Destin's Hold**…
The fight to save Earth has just begun…

If you loved this story by me (S.E. Smith) please leave a review. You can also take a look at additional books and sign up for my newsletter at **http://sesmithfl.com** to hear about my latest releases or keep in touch using the following links:

Website: http://sesmithfl.com
Newsletter: http://sesmithfl.com/?s=newsletter
Facebook: https://www.facebook.com/se.smith.5
Twitter: https://twitter.com/sesmithfl
Pinterest: http://www.pinterest.com/sesmithfl/
Blog: http://sesmithfl.com/blog/
Forum: http://www.sesmithromance.com/forum/

Excerpts of S.E. Smith Books

If you would like to read more S.E. Smith stories, she recommends Touch of Frost, the first in her Magic, New Mexico series. Or if you prefer a Paranormal or Western with a twist, you can check out Lily's Cowboys or Indiana Wild…

Additional Books by S.E. Smith

Short Stories and Novellas

For the Love of Tia
(Dragon Lords of Valdier Book 4.1)
A Dragonling's Easter
(Dragonlings of Valdier Book 1.1)
A Dragonling's Haunted Halloween
(Dragonlings of Valdier Book 1.2)
A Dragonling's Magical Christmas
(Dragonlings of Valdier Book 1.3)
A Warrior's Heart
(Marastin Dow Warriors Book 1.1)
Rescuing Mattie
(Lords of Kassis: Book 3.1)

Science Fiction/Paranormal Novels

Cosmos' Gateway Series

Tink's Neverland
(Cosmos' Gateway: Book 1)
Hannah's Warrior
(Cosmos' Gateway: Book 2)
Tansy's Titan
(Cosmos' Gateway: Book 3)
Cosmos' Promise
(Cosmos' Gateway: Book 4)

Merrick's Maiden
(Cosmos' Gateway Book 5)

Curizan Warrior Series

Ha'ven's Song
(Curizan Warrior: Book 1)

Dragon Lords of Valdier Series

Abducting Abby
(Dragon Lords of Valdier: Book 1)

Capturing Cara
(Dragon Lords of Valdier: Book 2)

Tracking Trisha
(Dragon Lords of Valdier: Book 3)

Ambushing Ariel
(Dragon Lords of Valdier: Book 4)

Cornering Carmen
(Dragon Lords of Valdier: Book 5)

Paul's Pursuit
(Dragon Lords of Valdier: Book 6)

Twin Dragons
(Dragon Lords of Valdier: Book 7)

Jaguin's Love
(Dragon Lords of Valdier: Book 8)

The Old Dragon of the Mountain's Christmas
(Dragon Lords of Valdier: Book 9)

Lords of Kassis Series

River's Run
(Lords of Kassis: Book 1)

Star's Storm
(Lords of Kassis: Book 2)

Jo's Journey
(Lords of Kassis: Book 3)

Ristéard's Unwilling Empress
(Lords of Kassis: Book 4)

<u>**Magic, New Mexico Series**</u>

Touch of Frost

(Magic, New Mexico Book 1)

Taking on Tory

(Magic, New Mexico Book 2)

<u>**Sarafin Warriors**</u>

Choosing Riley

(Sarafin Warriors: Book 1)

Viper's Defiant Mate

(Sarafin Warriors Book 2)

<u>**The Alliance Series**</u>

Hunter's Claim

(The Alliance: Book 1)

Razor's Traitorous Heart

(The Alliance: Book 2)

Dagger's Hope

(The Alliance: Book 3)

Challenging Saber

(The Alliance: Book 4)

<u>**Zion Warriors Series**</u>

Gracie's Touch

(Zion Warriors: Book 1)

Krac's Firebrand

(Zion Warriors: Book 2)

Paranormal and Time Travel Novels

<u>**Spirit Pass Series**</u>

Indiana Wild

(Spirit Pass: Book 1)

Spirit Warrior

(Spirit Pass Book 2)

<u>**Second Chance Series**</u>

Lily's Cowboys

(Second Chance: Book 1)

Touching Rune
(Second Chance: Book 2)

Young Adult Novels

Breaking Free Series

Voyage of the Defiance
(Breaking Free: Book 1)

Recommended Reading Order Lists:

http://sesmithfl.com/reading-list-by-events/
http://sesmithfl.com/reading-list-by-series/

About S.E. Smith

S.E. Smith is a ***New York Times, USA TODAY, International, and Award-Winning*** Bestselling author of science fiction, fantasy, paranormal, and contemporary works for adults, young adults, and children. She enjoys writing a wide variety of genres that pull her readers into worlds that take them away.

More great Scifi stories to sink your teeth into!
Reprinted with permission from the authors:

Eric 754: Cyborgs, Mankind Redefined Book 4
By Donna McDonald
www.donnamcdonaldauthor.com/eric-754

He often forgets he's a cyborg. All she sees in the mirror is a killing machine.

Marine Lance Corporal Eric Anderson tended to forget he was cyborg. Hell--most of the time he didn't give being mostly a military machine any thought. He'd always lived by his human gut, not his logic chip, so thinking out of the cybernetic box was just how he worked.

Then he met her--Evelyn 489--a female cyborg so erratic and dangerous she has to be kept locked away. Angry, violent, and full of deadly intentions, she epitomizes every fear about cyber scientists that ever kept him awake at night. Some warped cyber scientist stripped away her real identity to create the perfect female companion. And from what Eric can tell, he succeeded. But until he gave into his urge to be her hero, the woman didn't know she used to be Army Captain Lucille Evelyn Pennington.

Though Peyton is full of doubts, Eric is compelled to help Kyra and Nero restore the woman who once liked to be called Lucy. It doesn't help his cause that several people seem determined to kill her.

www.donnamcdonaldauthor.com/eric-754

Alliance: A Time Walker Novel
M. L. Callahan
http://www.mlcallahan.com/

For centuries aliens have waged a covert war for control of Earth using time travel as a weapon. A select group of humans become their soldiers, genetically modified pawns destined to be caught in the crossfire…

When Alexa's car is pushed over the edge of the Pacific Coast Highway, she fears Death has come for her. Instead, she is recruited by alien time travelers who want her to work for them. The aliens give her a mission; go back in time and eliminate the threat of a global pandemic. They've linked the plague to one sexy and intriguing man, Luke Lawson.

Luke Lawson is a scientist, not a spy, but he finds himself trapped working on a classified project. They ask him to create a vaccine for an engineered virus, and he accepts the challenge. But this virus is like nothing he's ever seen before, it's strange, almost...alien. This virus will wipe out human life as we know it. As far as he's concerned, he doesn't have a choice. He's the only one who can figure out how to stop it.

When Alexa shows up claiming his research is going to wipe out most of the world's population, Luke must make a decision…is the sexy woman in front of him is telling him the truth, or completely insane? Too bad simply agreeing to help the beautiful woman won't be enough. The virus's creation was no accident. Alexa's aliens aren't the only players in the game, and they didn't travel through time alone. An immortal enemy wants all of the Timewalkers dead, and Alexa is first on his list.

Join Luke and Alexa for an action-packed, sexy rollercoaster ride as they struggle between love and hate, good and evil, warring alien factions, secret government agencies, and a love so strong they will risk everything they are to save it.

TEASER:
He closed the distance between them like closing a zipper until their mouths were nearly touching. Every move was slow. Deliberate. Her lips were millimeters from his own, still he waited. She savored the contact. Enjoyed the soft push of her breasts against his firm chest. The moist heat of their mouths mingled in the air between them.
"Luke?" She whispered his name against his lips, acutely aware of the turned-down bed just steps away. Her mind was wicked tonight. She should be figuring out how to destroy the virus and save the world.

Instead, all she could think about was getting Luke naked in that bed. She wanted him, skin to skin. She wanted to drown in his scent and revel in the glide of skin on skin. She wanted him inside her, kissing her, touching her everywhere. Making her whimper and beg, making her forget.

Facebook: https://www.facebook.com/AuthorMLCallahan
Twitter: https://twitter.com/ml_callahan
Website: http://mlcallahan.com

CPSIA information can be obtained
at www.ICGtesting.com
Printed in the USA
BVOW11s1109160316
440566BV00025B/412/P